The Adventure of
Mata Hari's Harem

A New Sherlock Holmes Mystery

Craig Stephen Copland

Published by:

Conservative Growth Inc.
3104 30th Avenue, Suite 427
Vernon, British Columbia, Canada
V1T 9M9

Cover design by Rita Toews

ISBN: 9798492514891

2023 ev ΘΕλημα Anno CXIX Θin ℔ FRATER KEALLACH 93/676
2024 ev Anno CXX Θin ♈

The Adventure of
Mata Hari's Harem

A New Sherlock Holmes Mystery

Note to Readers:

This new story is a sequel to the original Sherlock Holmes story, His Last Bow

Your enjoyment of this new story will be greatly enhanced by your familiarity with the original.

It has therefore been added to the text as a preface.

NEWAEON PRODUCTIONS

G.M.Kelly, Editor, The Newaeon Newsletter
1001 New Brighton Rd, #510, Pittsburgh, PA 15202
Castle of the Silver Star: www.gmkelly.com
E-mail: gmkelly93@comcast.net

Dedication

As a Canadian writer, I dedicate this story to the memory of the 59,544 Canadian soldiers who died during the Great War and the over 172,000 who were wounded. Their sacrifice can never be forgotten.

If you enjoy this story or if there are ways it could be improved, please help the author and future readers by leaving a constructive review on the site from which you obtained the book. Thank you. Much appreciated,

CSC

Contents

Acknowledgements

All writers of Sherlock Holmes pastiches or fan-fiction are indebted to Arthur Conan Doyle for his creation of Sherlock Holmes and the writing of The Canon.

Friends and fellow writers in the English Writers of Buenos Aires and the Vernon, British Columbia, Writers' Critique Group all endured many chapters of this story. Their suggestions were invaluable in improving the story.

I must also pay tribute to my wife, Mary Engelking, my older brother, Jim Copland, my writing and lunch buddy, Geoff White, and Cheryl Adamkiewicz, a splendid copy editor, for their reading and editing of the story.

There are many biographies of Margaretha Zelle MacLeod—known to the world as Mata Hari. If you wish to know more about the life of this unusual woman, I recommend *A Tangled Web,* by Mary Craig and *Femme Fatale* by Pat Shipman. I enjoyed and learned from both of them.

There are many excellent books recounting the opening days of World War One. In doing the necessary research for this story, I read and learned from parts of *Catastrophe* by Max Hastings, *To Hell and Back* by Ian Kershaw, *The Great War* by Peter Hart, *The Great Retreat of 1914* by Spencer Jones, and from my favorite Canadian historian, Margaret Macmillan, who wrote *The War That Ended Peace.* All these books are recommended to anyone wanting to learn more about the fateful days of the summer of 1914.

I wrote this story while spending a delightful three hours a week attending classes at the University of British Columbia – Okanagan Campus. There I sat in on illuminating lectures given by Professor Todd Campbell on the period of history from 1900 to 1939. The events covered in this story took place during those years, and I am grateful for Dr. Campbell's insights.

Some of the earliest spy stories of World War One were written by John Buchan. I borrowed some wonderful material from *Greenmantle.*

A special note of appreciation is extended to Mr. Steve O'Hara of Castleford West, Yorkshire, for volunteering to serve as one of the characters in this story.

I have a personal connection to Mata Hari.

July 1964. I was a camper at a Bible Camp — Camp Mini-Yo-We in Muskoka, Ontario, Canada. Each cabin of boys in the senior section (Northwoods) was required to come up with a name for ourselves. My cabin chose something boring and typical like 'Lumberjacks' (Don't worry, it was before Monty Python altered the image of Lumberjacks forever). But another cabin, obviously more creative and sophisticated than the one I was in (and perhaps hornier), named themselves MATA HARI'S HAREM. At the time, I had no idea who Mata Hari was, and I can only assume that the counselors who allowed them to keep that name didn't either. In retrospect, it now seems very strange that a cabin of teenage boys at a Bible camp affiliated with the ultra-conservative sect, the Plymouth Brethren, were permitted to identify themselves as the consorts of a woman who, in her day, was world-famous as an erotic/exotic/nearly-nude dancer, as the costly courtesan of a long line of rich and powerful men, and who was executed by the French during World War One as a spy. Who knew? But the name of that exceptional woman and her adolescent worshippers has stuck with me. Finally, I got to use it again. But credit where it is due: to Bible camp in 1964.

Note to Readers

(please read)

Each of the New Sherlock Holmes Mysteries is a tribute to one of the original stories in The Canon. This one was inspired by *His Last* H *Bow.*

However, it is not only a tribute. It is written as an immediate sequel to that story, picking up where that one ended on the night of the second of August, 1914. There are many direct connections to the original story. Your enjoyment of the new story will be enhanced by your being familiar with *His Last Bow*. For that reason, I have affixed the original story to this one as a preface.

If you are already familiar with the original Sherlock Holmes story, please advance to Chapter One of the new story.

Almost all the other stories in The Canon are recounted by Dr. Watson and written in the first person. *His Last Bow* was written in the third person by an unnamed narrator. In keeping with the style of the original, this new story is also written in the third person. Any and all suggestions for improvement are more than welcome.

A Note from
John H. Watson, MD

The friends of Mr. Sherlock Holmes will be glad to learn that he is still alive and well, though somewhat crippled by occasional attacks of rheumatism. He has, for many years, lived in a small farm upon the Downs five miles from Eastbourne, where his time is divided between philosophy and agriculture. During this period of rest, he has refused the most princely offers to take up various cases, having determined that his retirement was a permanent one. The approach of the German war caused him, however, to lay his remarkable combination of intellectual and practical activity at the disposal of the Government, with historical results which are recounted in *His Last Bow*. Several previous experiences which have lain long in my portfolio have been added to *His Last Bow* so as to complete the volume.

John H. Watson, M.D.

Preface

His Last Bow:

The War Service of Sherlock Holmes

It was nine o'clock at night upon the second of August—the most terrible August in the history of the world. One might have thought already that God's curse hung heavy over a degenerate world, for there was an awesome hush and a feeling of vague expectancy in the sultry and stagnant air. The sun had long set, but one blood-red gash like an open wound lay low in the distant west. Above, the stars were shining brightly, and below, the lights of the shipping glimmered in the bay. The two famous Germans stood beside the stone parapet of the garden walk, with the long, low, heavily gabled house behind them, and they looked down upon the broad sweep of the beach at the foot of the great chalk cliff in which Von Bork, like some wandering eagle, had perched himself four years before. They stood with their heads close together, talking

1

in low, confidential tones. From below the two glowing ends of their cigars might have been the smoldering eyes of some malignant fiend looking down in the darkness.

A remarkable man this Von Bork—a man who could hardly be matched among all the devoted agents of the Kaiser. It was his talents which had first recommended him for the English mission, the most important mission of all, but since he had taken it over those talents had become more and more manifest to the half-dozen people in the world who were really in touch with the truth. One of these was his present companion, Baron Von Herling, the chief secretary of the legation, whose huge 100-horse-power Benz car was blocking the country lane as it waited to waft its owner back to London.

"So far as I can judge the trend of events, you will probably be back in Berlin within the week," the secretary was saying. "When you get there, my dear Von Bork, I think you will be surprised at the welcome you will receive. I happen to know what is thought in the highest quarters of your work in this country." He was a huge man, the secretary, deep, broad, and tall, with a slow, heavy fashion of speech which had been his main asset in his political career.

Von Bork laughed.

"They are not very hard to deceive," he remarked. "A more docile, simple folk could not be imagined."

"I don't know about that," said the other thoughtfully. "They have strange limits and one must learn to observe them. It is that surface simplicity of theirs which makes a trap for the stranger. One's first impression is that they are entirely soft. Then one comes suddenly upon something very hard, and you know that you have reached the limit and must adapt yourself to the fact. They have, for example, their insular conventions which simply *must* be observed."

"Meaning 'good form' and that sort of thing?" Von Bork sighed as one who had suffered much.

"Meaning British prejudice in all its queer manifestations. As an example, I may quote one of my own worst blunders—I can afford to talk of my blunders, for you know my work well enough to be aware of my successes. It was on my first arrival. I was invited to a week-end gathering at the country house of a cabinet minister. The conversation was amazingly indiscreet."

Von Bork nodded. "I've been there," said he dryly.

"Exactly. Well, I naturally sent a résumé of the information to Berlin. Unfortunately our good chancellor is a little heavy-handed in these matters, and he transmitted a remark which showed that he was aware of what had been said. This, of course, took the trail straight up to me. You've no idea the harm that it did me. There was nothing soft about our British hosts on that occasion, I can assure you. I was two years living it down. Now you, with this sporting pose of yours—"

"No, no, don't call it a pose. A pose is an artificial thing. This is quite natural. I am a born sportsman. I enjoy it."

"Well, that makes it the more effective. You yacht against them, you hunt with them, you play polo, you match them in every game, your four-in-hand takes the prize at Olympia. I have even heard that you go the length of boxing with the young officers. What is the result? Nobody takes you seriously. You are a 'good old sport' 'quite a decent fellow for a German,' a hard-drinking, night-club, knock-about-town, devil-may-care young fellow. And all the time this quiet country house of yours is the centre of half the mischief in England, and the sporting squire the most astute secret-service man in Europe. Genius, my dear Von Bork—genius!"

"You flatter me, Baron. But certainly I may claim my four years in this country have not been unproductive. I've never shown you my little store. Would you mind stepping in for a moment?"

The door of the study opened straight on to the terrace. Von Bork pushed it back, and, leading the way, he clicked the switch of the electric light. He then closed the door behind the bulky form which followed him and carefully adjusted the heavy curtain over the latticed window. Only when all these precautions had been taken and tested did he turn his sunburned aquiline face to his guest.

"Some of my papers have gone," said he. "When my wife and the household left yesterday for Flushing, they took the less important with them. I must, of course, claim the protection of the embassy for the others."

"Your name has already been filed as one of the personal suites. There will be no difficulties for you or your baggage. Of course, it is just possible that we may not have to go. England may leave France to her fate. We are sure that there is no binding treaty between them."

"And Belgium?"

"Yes, and Belgium, too."

Von Bork shook his head. "I don't see how that could be. There is a definite treaty there. She could never recover from such a humiliation."

"She would at least have peace for the moment."

"But her honour?"

"Tut, my dear sir, we live in a utilitarian age. Honour is a medieval conception. Besides England is not ready. It is an inconceivable thing, but even our special war tax of fifty million, which one would think made our purpose as clear as if we had advertised it on the front page of the *Times*, has not roused these people from their slumbers. Here and there one hears a question. It is my business to find an answer. Here and there also there is an irritation. It is my business to soothe it. But I can assure you that so far as the essentials go—the storage of munitions, the preparation for submarine attack, the arrangements for making high explosives—nothing is prepared. How, then, can England come in, especially when we have stirred her up such a devil's brew of Irish civil war, window-breaking Furies, and God knows what to keep her thoughts at home."

"She must think of her future."

"Ah, that is another matter. I fancy that in the future we have our own very definite plans about England, and that your information will be very vital to us. It is to-day or to-morrow with Mr. John Bull. If he prefers to-day we are perfectly ready. If it is to-morrow we shall be more ready still. I should think they would be wiser to fight with allies than without them, but that is their own affair. This week is their week of destiny. But you were speaking of your papers." He sat in the armchair with the light shining upon his broad bald head, while he puffed sedately at his cigar.

The large oak-panelled, book-lined room had a curtain hung in the further corner. When this was drawn it disclosed a large, brass-bound safe. Von Bork detached a small key from his watch chain, and after some considerable manipulation of the lock he swung open the heavy door.

"Look!" said he, standing clear, with a wave of his hand.

The light shone vividly into the opened safe, and the secretary of the embassy gazed with an absorbed interest at the rows of stuffed pigeon-holes with which it was furnished. Each pigeon-hole had its label, and his eyes as he glanced along them read a long series of such titles as "Fords," "Harbour-defences," "Aeroplanes," "Ireland," "Egypt," "Portsmouth forts," "The Channel," "Rosythe," and a score of others. Each compartment was bristling with papers and plans.

"Colossal!" said the secretary. Putting down his cigar he softly clapped his fat hands.

"And all in four years, Baron. Not such a bad show for the hard-drinking, hard-riding country squire. But the gem of my collection is coming and there is the setting all ready for it." He pointed to a space over which "Naval Signals" was printed.

"But you have a good dossier there already."

"Out of date and waste paper. The Admiralty in some way got the alarm and every code has been changed. It was a blow, Baron— the worst setback in my whole campaign. But thanks to my check-book and the good Altamont all will be well to-night."

The Baron looked at his watch and gave a guttural exclamation of disappointment.

"Well, I really can wait no longer. You can imagine that things are moving at present in Carlton Terrace and that we have all to be at our posts. I had hoped to be able to bring news of your great coup. Did Altamont name no hour?"

Von Bork pushed over a telegram.

Will come without fail to-night and bring new sparking plugs.—ALTAMONT.

"Sparking plugs, eh?"

"You see he poses as a motor expert and I keep a full garage. In our code everything likely to come up is named after some spare part. If he talks of a radiator, it is a battleship, of an oil pump a cruiser, and so on. Sparking plugs are naval signals."

"From Portsmouth at midday," said the secretary, examining the superscription. "By the way, what do you give him?"

"Five hundred pounds for this particular job. Of course, he has a salary as well."

"The greedy rogue. They are useful, these traitors, but I grudge them their blood money."

"I grudge Altamont nothing. He is a wonderful worker. If I pay him well, at least he delivers the goods, to use his own phrase. Besides he is not a traitor. I assure you that our most pan-Germanic Junker is a sucking dove in his feelings towards England as compared with a real bitter Irish-American."

"Oh, an Irish-American?"

"If you heard him talk you would not doubt it. Sometimes I assure you I can hardly understand him. He seems to have declared war on the King's English as well as on the English king. Must you really go? He may be here any moment."

"No. I'm sorry, but I have already overstayed my time. We shall expect you early to-morrow, and when you get that signal book through the little door on the Duke of York's steps you can put a triumphant Finis to your record in England. What! Tokay!" He indicated a heavily sealed dust-covered bottle which stood with two high glasses upon a salver.

"May I offer you a glass before your journey?"

"No, thanks. But it looks like revelry."

"Altamont has a nice taste in wines, and he took a fancy to my Tokay. He is a touchy fellow and needs humouring in small things. I have to study him, I assure you." They had strolled out on to the terrace again, and along it to the further end where at a touch from the Baron's chauffeur the great car shivered and chuckled. "Those are the lights of Harwich, I suppose," said the secretary, pulling on his dust coat. "How still and peaceful it all seems. There may be other lights within the week, and the English coast a less tranquil place! The heavens, too, may not be quite so peaceful if all that the good Zepplin promises us comes true. By the way, who is that?"

Only one window showed a light behind them; in it there stood a lamp, and beside it, seated at a table, was a dear old ruddy-faced woman in a country cap. She was bending over her knitting and stopping occasionally to stroke a large black cat upon a stool beside her.

"That is Martha, the only servant I have left."

The secretary chuckled.

"She might almost personify Britannia," said he, "with her complete self-absorption and general air of comfortable somnolence. Well, au revoir, Von Bork!" With a final wave of his hand, he sprang into the car, and a moment later the two golden cones from the headlights shot through the darkness. The secretary lay back in the cushions of the luxurious limousine, with his thoughts so full of the impending European tragedy that he hardly observed that as his car swung round the village street it nearly passed over a little Ford coming in the opposite direction.

Von Bork walked slowly back to the study when the last gleams of the motor lamps had faded into the distance. As he passed he observed that his old housekeeper had put out her lamp and retired. It was a new experience to him, the silence and darkness of his widespread house, for his family and household had been a large one. It was a relief to him, however, to think that they were all in safety and that, but for that one old woman who had lingered in the kitchen, he had the whole place to himself. There was a good deal of tidying up to do inside his study and he set himself to do it until his keen, handsome face was flushed with the heat of the burning papers. A leather valise stood beside his table, and into this he began to pack very neatly and systematically the precious contents of his safe. He had hardly got started with the work, however, when his quick ears caught the sounds of a distant car. Instantly he gave an exclamation of satisfaction, strapped up the valise, shut the safe, locked it, and hurried out on to the terrace. He was just in time to see the lights of a small car come to a halt at the gate. A passenger sprang out of it and advanced swiftly towards him, while the chauffeur, a heavily built, elderly man with a grey moustache, settled down like one who resigns himself to a long vigil.

"Well?" asked Von Bork eagerly, running forward to meet his visitor.

For answer the man waved a small brown-paper parcel triumphantly above his head.

"You can give me the glad hand to-night, mister," he cried. "I'm bringing home the bacon at last."

"The signals?"

"Same as I said in my cable. Every last one of them, semaphore, lamp code, Marconi—a copy, mind you, not the original. That was too dangerous. But it's the real goods, and you can lay to that." He slapped the German upon the shoulder with a rough familiarity from which the other winced.

"Come in," he said. "I'm all alone in the house. I was only waiting for this. Of course a copy is better than the original. If an original were missing, they would change the whole thing. You think it's all safe about the copy?"

The Irish-American had entered the study and stretched his long limbs from the armchair. He was a tall, gaunt man of sixty, with clear-cut features and a small goatee beard which gave him a general resemblance to the caricatures of Uncle Sam. A half-smoked, sodden cigar hung from the corner of his mouth, and as he sat down, he struck a match and relit it. "Making ready for a move?" he remarked as he looked round him. "Say, mister," he added, as his eyes fell upon the safe from which the curtain was now removed, "you don't tell me you keep your papers in that?"

"Why not?"

"Gosh, in a wide-open contraption like that! And they reckon you to be some spy. Why, a Yankee crook would be into that with a can-opener. If I'd known that any letter of mine was goin' to lie loose in a thing like that, I'd have been a mug to write to you at all."

"It would puzzle any crook to force that safe," Von Bork answered. "You won't cut that metal with any tool."

"But the lock?"

"No, it's a double combination lock. You know what that is?"

"Search me," said the American.

"Well, you need a word as well as a set of figures before you can get the lock to work." He rose and showed a double-radiating disc round the keyhole. "This outer one is for the letters, the inner one for the figures."

"Well, well, that's fine."

"So it's not quite as simple as you thought. It was four years ago that I had it made, and what do you think I chose for the word and figures?"

"It's beyond me."

"Well, I chose August for the word, and 1914 for the figures, and here we are."

The American's face showed his surprise and admiration.

"My, but that was smart! You had it down to a fine thing."

"Yes, a few of us even then could have guessed the date. Here it is, and I'm shutting down to-morrow morning."

"Well, I guess you'll have to fix me up also. I'm not staying in this goldarned country all on my lonesome. In a week or less, from what I see, John Bull will be on his hind legs and fair ramping. I'd rather watch him from over the water."

"But you're an American citizen?"

"Well, so was Jack James an American citizen, but he's doing time in Portland all the same. It cuts no ice with a British copper to tell him you're an American citizen. 'It's British law and order over here,' says he. By the way, mister, talking of Jack James, it seems to me you don't do much to cover your men."

"What do you mean?" Von Bork asked sharply.

"Well, you are their employer, ain't you? It's up to you to see that they don't fall down. But they do fall down, and when did you ever pick them up? There's James—"

"It was James's own fault. You know that yourself. He was too self-willed for the job."

"James was a bonehead—I give you that. Then there was Hollis."

"The man was mad."

"Well, he went a bit woozy towards the end. It's enough to make a man bug-house when he has to play a part from morning to night with a hundred guys all ready to set the coppers wise to him. But now there is Steiner—"

Von Bork started violently, and his ruddy face turned a shade paler.

"What about Steiner?"

"Well, they've got him, that's all. They raided his store last night, and he and his papers are all in Portsmouth jail. You'll go off and he, poor devil, will have to stand the racket, and lucky if he gets off with his life. That's why I want to get over the water as soon as you do."

Von Bork was a strong, self-contained man, but it was easy to see that the news had shaken him.

"How could they have got on to Steiner?" he muttered. "That's the worst blow yet."

"Well, you nearly had a worse one, for I believe they are not far off me."

"You don't mean that!"

"Sure thing. My landlady down Fratton way had some inquiries, and when I heard of it I guessed it was time for me to hustle. But what I want to know, mister, is how the coppers know these things? Steiner is the fifth man you've lost since I signed on with you, and I know the name of the sixth if I don't get a move on. How do you explain it, and ain't you ashamed to see your men go down like this?"

Von Bork flushed crimson.

"How dare you speak in such a way!"

"If I didn't dare things, mister, I wouldn't be in your service. But I'll tell you straight what is in my mind. I've heard that with you German politicians when an agent has done his work you are not sorry to see him put away."

Von Bork sprang to his feet.

"Do you dare to suggest that I have given away my own agents!"

"I don't stand for that, mister, but there's a stool pigeon or a cross somewhere, and it's up to you to find out where it is. Anyhow I am taking no more chances. It's me for little Holland, and the sooner the better."

Von Bork had mastered his anger.

"We have been allies too long to quarrel now at the very hour of victory," he said. "You've done splendid work and taken risks, and I can't forget it. By all means go to Holland, and you can get a boat from Rotterdam to New York. No other line will be safe a week from now. I'll take that book and pack it with the rest."

The American held the small parcel in his hand, but made no motion to give it up.

"What about the dough?" he asked.

"The what?"

"The boodle. The reward. The £500. The gunner turned damned nasty at the last, and I had to square him with an extra hundred dollars or it would have been nitsky for you and me. 'Nothin' doin'!' says he, and he meant it, too, but the last hundred did it. It's cost me two hundred pound from first to last, so it isn't likely I'd give it up without gettin' my wad."

Von Bork smiled with some bitterness. "You don't seem to have a very high opinion of my honour," said he, "you want the money before you give up the book."

"Well, mister, it is a business proposition."

"All right. Have your way." He sat down at the table and scribbled a check, which he tore from the book, but he refrained from handing it to his companion. "After all, since we are to be on such terms, Mr. Altamont," said he, "I don't see why I should trust you any more than you trust me. Do you understand?" he added, looking back over his shoulder at the American. "There's the check upon the table. I claim the right to examine that parcel before you pick the money up."

The American passed it over without a word. Von Bork undid a winding of string and two wrappers of paper. Then he sat gazing for a moment in silent amazement at a small blue book which lay before him. Across the cover was printed in golden letters *Practical Handbook of Bee Culture*. Only for one instant did the master spy glare at this strangely irrelevant inscription. The next he was gripped at the back of his neck by a grasp of iron, and a chloroformed sponge was held in front of his writhing face.

"Another glass, Watson!" said Mr. Sherlock Holmes as he extended the bottle of Imperial Tokay.

The thickset chauffeur, who had seated himself by the table, pushed forward his glass with some eagerness.

"It is a good wine, Holmes."

"A remarkable wine, Watson. Our friend upon the sofa has assured me that it is from Franz Josef's special cellar at the Schoenbrunn Palace. Might I trouble you to open the window, for chloroform vapour does not help the palate."

The safe was ajar, and Holmes standing in front of it was removing dossier after dossier, swiftly examining each, and then packing it neatly in Von Bork's valise. The German lay upon the sofa sleeping stertorously with a strap round his upper arms and another round his legs.

"We need not hurry ourselves, Watson. We are safe from interruption. Would you mind touching the bell? There is no one in the house except old Martha, who has played her part to admiration. I got her the situation here when first I took the matter up. Ah, Martha, you will be glad to hear that all is well."

The pleasant old lady had appeared in the doorway. She curtseyed with a smile to Mr. Holmes, but glanced with some apprehension at the figure upon the sofa.

"It is all right, Martha. He has not been hurt at all."

"I am glad of that, Mr. Holmes. According to his lights he has been a kind master. He wanted me to go with his wife to Germany yesterday, but that would hardly have suited your plans, would it, sir?"

"No, indeed, Martha. So long as you were here, I was easy in my mind. We waited some time for your signal to-night."

"It was the secretary, sir."

"I know. His car passed ours."

"I thought he would never go. I knew that it would not suit your plans, sir, to find him here."

"No, indeed. Well, it only meant that we waited half an hour or so until I saw your lamp go out and knew that the coast was clear. You can report to me to-morrow in London, Martha, at Claridge's Hotel."

"Very good, sir."

"I suppose you have everything ready to leave."

"Yes, sir. He posted seven letters to-day. I have the addresses as usual."

"Very good, Martha. I will look into them to-morrow. Good-night. These papers," he continued as the old lady vanished, "are not of very great importance, for, of course, the information which they represent has been sent off long ago to the German government. These are the originals which could not safely be got out of the country."

"Then they are of no use."

"I should not go so far as to say that, Watson. They will at least show our people what is known and what is not. I may say that a good many of these papers have come through me, and I need not add are thoroughly untrustworthy. It would brighten my declining years to see a German cruiser navigating the Solent according to the mine-field plans which I have furnished. But you, Watson"—he stopped his work and took his old friend by the shoulders—"I've hardly seen you in the light yet. How have the years used you? You look the same blithe boy as ever."

"I feel twenty years younger, Holmes. I have seldom felt so happy as when I got your wire asking me to meet you at Harwich with the car. But you, Holmes—you have changed very little—save for that horrible goatee."

"These are the sacrifices one makes for one's country, Watson," said Holmes, pulling at his little tuft. "To-morrow it will be but a dreadful memory. With my hair cut and a few other superficial changes I shall no doubt reappear at Claridge's to-morrow as I was before this American stunt—I beg your pardon, Watson, my well of English seems to be permanently defiled—before this American job came my way."

"But you have retired, Holmes. We heard of you as living the life of a hermit among your bees and your books in a small farm upon the South Downs."

"Exactly, Watson. Here is the fruit of my leisured ease, the magnum opus of my latter years!" He picked up the volume from the table and read out the whole title, *Practical Handbook of Bee Culture, with Some Observations upon the Segregation of the Queen*. "Alone I did it. Behold the fruit of pensive nights and laborious days when I watched the little working gangs as once I watched the criminal world of London."

"But how did you get to work again?"

"Ah, I have often marvelled at it myself. The Foreign Minister alone I could have withstood, but when the Premier also deigned to visit my humble roof—! The fact is, Watson, that this gentleman upon the sofa was a bit too good for our people. He was in a class by himself. Things were going wrong, and no one could understand why they were going wrong. Agents were suspected or even caught, but there was evidence of some strong and secret central force. It was absolutely necessary to expose it. Strong pressure was brought upon me to look into the matter. It has cost me two years, Watson, but they have not been devoid of excitement. When I say that I started my pilgrimage at Chicago, graduated in an Irish secret society at Buffalo, gave serious trouble to the constabulary at Skibbareen, and so eventually caught the eye of a subordinate agent of Von Bork, who recommended me as a likely man, you will realise that the matter was complex. Since then I have been honoured by his confidence, which has not prevented most of his plans going subtly wrong and five of his best agents being in prison. I watched them, Watson, and I picked them as they ripened. Well, sir, I hope that you are none the worse!"

The last remark was addressed to Von Bork himself, who after much gasping and blinking had lain quietly listening to Holmes's statement. He broke out now into a furious stream of German invective, his face convulsed with passion. Holmes continued his swift investigation of documents while his prisoner cursed and swore.

"Though unmusical, German is the most expressive of all languages," he observed when Von Bork had stopped from pure exhaustion. "Hullo! Hullo!" he added as he looked hard at the corner of a tracing before putting it in the box. "This should put another bird in the cage. I had no idea that the paymaster was such a rascal, though I have long had an eye upon him. Mister Von Bork, you have a great deal to answer for."

The prisoner had raised himself with some difficulty upon the sofa and was staring with a strange mixture of amazement and hatred at his captor.

"I shall get level with you, Altamont," he said, speaking with slow deliberation. "If it takes me all my life, I shall get level with you!"

"The old sweet song," said Holmes. "How often have I heard it in days gone by. It was a favorite ditty of the late lamented Professor Moriarty. Colonel Sebastian Moran has also been known to warble it. And yet I live and keep bees upon the South Downs."

"Curse you, you double traitor!" cried the German, straining against his bonds and glaring murder from his furious eyes.

"No, no, it is not so bad as that," said Holmes, smiling. "As my speech surely shows you, Mr. Altamont of Chicago had no existence in fact. I used him and he is gone."

"Then who are you?"

"It is really immaterial who I am, but since the matter seems to interest you, Mr. Von Bork, I may say that this is not my first acquaintance with the members of your family. I have done a good deal of business in Germany in the past and my name is probably familiar to you."

"I would wish to know it," said the Prussian grimly.

"It was I who brought about the separation between Irene Adler and the late King of Bohemia when your cousin Heinrich was the Imperial Envoy. It was I also who saved from murder, by the Nihilist Klopman, Count Von und Zu Grafenstein, who was your mother's elder brother. It was I—"

Von Bork sat up in amazement.

"There is only one man," he cried.

"Exactly," said Holmes.

Von Bork groaned and sank back on the sofa. "And most of that information came through you," he cried. "What is it worth? What have I done? It is my ruin forever!"

"It is certainly a little untrustworthy," said Holmes. "It will require some checking and you have little time to check it. Your admiral may find the new guns rather larger than he expects, and the cruisers perhaps a trifle faster."

Von Bork clutched at his own throat in despair.

"There are a good many other points of detail which will, no doubt, come to light in good time. But you have one quality which is very rare in a German, Mr. Von Bork: you are a sportsman and you will bear me no ill-will when you realise that you, who have outwitted so many other people, have at last been outwitted yourself. After all, you have done your best for your country, and I have done my best for mine, and what could be more natural? Besides," he added, not unkindly, as he laid his hand upon the shoulder of the prostrate man, "it is better than to fall before some ignoble foe. These papers are now ready, Watson. If you will help me with our prisoner, I think that we may get started for London at once."

It was no easy task to move Von Bork, for he was a strong and a desperate man. Finally, holding either arm, the two friends walked him very slowly down the garden walk which he had trod with such proud confidence when he received the congratulations of the famous diplomatist only a few hours before. After a short, final struggle he was hoisted, still bound hand and foot, into the spare seat of the little car. His precious valise was wedged in beside him.

"I trust that you are as comfortable as circumstances permit," said Holmes when the final arrangements were made. "Should I be guilty of a liberty if I lit a cigar and placed it between your lips?"

But all amenities were wasted upon the angry German.

"I suppose you realise, Mr. Sherlock Holmes," said he, "that if your government bears you out in this treatment it becomes an act of war."

"What about your government and all this treatment?" said Holmes, tapping the valise.

"You are a private individual. You have no warrant for my arrest. The whole proceeding is absolutely illegal and outrageous."

"Absolutely," said Holmes.

"Kidnapping a German subject."

"And stealing his private papers."

"Well, you realise your position, you and your accomplice here. If I were to shout for help as we pass through the village—"

"My dear sir, if you did anything so foolish you would probably enlarge the two limited titles of our village inns by giving us 'The Dangling Prussian' as a signpost. The Englishman is a patient creature, but at present his temper is a little inflamed, and it would be as well not to try him too far. No, Mr. Von Bork, you will go with us in a quiet, sensible fashion to Scotland Yard, whence you can send for your friend, Baron Von Herling, and see if even now you may not fill that place which he has reserved for you in the ambassadorial suite. As to you, Watson, you are joining us with your old service, as I understand, so London won't be out of your way. Stand with me here upon the terrace, for it may be the last quiet talk that we shall ever have."

The two friends chatted in intimate converse for a few minutes, recalling once again the days of the past, while their prisoner vainly wriggled to undo the bonds that held him. As they turned to the car Holmes pointed back to the moonlit sea and shook a thoughtful head.

"There's an east wind coming, Watson."

"I think not, Holmes. It is very warm."

"Good old Watson! You are the one fixed point in a changing age. There's an east wind coming all the same, such a wind as never blew on England yet. It will be cold and bitter, Watson, and a good many of us may wither before its blast. But it's God's own wind none the less, and a cleaner, better, stronger land will lie in the sunshine when the storm has cleared. Start her up, Watson, for it's time that we were on our way. I have a check for five hundred pounds which should be cashed early, for the drawer is quite capable of stopping it if he can."

The Adventure of Mata Hari's Harem

The Continuing War Service of Sherlock Holmes

Partial Timeline of the Opening Days of the Great War

July 28: Austria-Hungary declares war on Serbia
Aug. 1: Germany and Russia declare war on each other
Aug. 2: Sherlock Holmes breaks up the von Bork spy network
Aug. 3: Germany and France declare war on each other
Aug. 4: Germany declares war on Belgium, United Kingdom declares war on Germany
Aug. 6: Austria-Hungary declares war on Russia, Serbia declares war on Germany
Aug. 12: United Kingdom and France declare war on Austria-Hungary
Aug 14-25: Battle of the Frontiers. French advances into Alsace and are pushed back by Germany
Aug. 22: Austria-Hungary declares war on Belgium
Aug. 23: Battle of Mons. BEF impedes the advance of the German army
Aug. 26: Battle of Tannenberg. Germany defeats Russia.
Aug. 28: Austria-Hungary declares war on Belgium
Sept. 5-12: 'Miracle of the Marne.' Allied forces stop German advance and counter attack.
Sept 12 – 21. Battle of the Aisne. German retreat halts. Trench warfare begins on the Western Front
Nov. 2: Russia and Serbia declare war on the Ottoman Empire
Nov. 5: United Kingdom and France declare war on the Ottoman Empire
December 1914 – August 1918. Trench warfare continues. Millions of lives lost on both sides.

Chapter One

To Whitehall with Von Bork

The lamps are going out all over Europe; we shall not see them lit again in our lifetime."

British Foreign Secretary Sir Edward Grey, August 1914

Dover, August 2, 1914

It was half-past eleven o'clock at night on the second of August, 1914.

Von Bork, the master German spy, was bound hand and foot and immobile in the back of the small Ford. The files from his safe, exposing the secrets gleaned by his network of spies, were securely held in a valise that would soon be handed over to the office of the Secret Intelligence Service. The task had taken Sherlock Holmes two years of undercover service as a spy, but now it was over. His work was completed. Finally, he could take his last bow.

"Well done, old friend," said Dr. Watson. "Your country would be terribly proud of you if only they were ever to learn about what you have done."

"Thank you, Watson," said Holmes. "It has been a long two years in America and then here. I am ready to call it quits. I have missed my books and my bees. And I have missed you, my dear Doctor."

"No more ingenious criminals to track down? No more evil networks to destroy?"

"No. I have made my contribution and, quite frankly, I find that I am now a man of well over sixty years, and I am weary."

Sherlock Holmes and Dr. John Watson stood atop the white cliffs of Dover gazing out over the Channel. A waxing gibbous moon had risen, and its shimmering path of light reflected off the ocean. A soft, night wind was blowing from the east. Somewhere beyond the dark horizon lay the coast of France.

"Has France declared war yet?" asked Watson.

"Not yet," said Holmes. "It is expected that they will by this time tomorrow."

"What about the Russians?"

"They went to war with Germany yesterday."

"What about us?"

"It has been over a hundred years since we sent English soldiers to fight in Europe. Pray God, England can keep out of the conflict, safe on our side of the Channel. But the signs are not promising."

"What are we going to do with Von Bork?" asked Watson.

"Drive him to London and deposit him at Whitehall."

"When?"

"Now."

"Could you spare a moment to shave off that silly goatee?"

"Later."

The two old friends chatted in intimate converse whilst in the rear seat of the motorcar Von Bork vainly struggled to undo the bonds that held him. Having enjoyed a few minutes recalling the days and adventures they shared in the past, they bade goodbye to the aging Martha, who had been so helpful to them and climbed into the small Ford. It was dark along the coast, and the roads were empty, but that was good. They had a slow but clear drive all the way to London.

It had gone two o'clock in the morning when they pulled up behind a wing of Whitehall. Two nondescript men in nondescript suits met them, and each took an end of Von Bork and carried him into the dark building. That was the last they or any member of the public would ever see the German spy. A few minutes later, a man in a colonel's uniform emerged from the building and met with Holmes and Watson under the glow of a street lamp.

"Well done, Mr. Altamont," he said and then laughed softly. "That is the moniker you have been going by for the past two years is it not, Mr. Holmes?"

"It is, Colonel Mountford. It served me well in Chicago and Buffalo. It was all I needed along with an Irish accent to fool the Germans. Did you wish to examine the trove of papers Von Bork brought with him—not voluntarily, of course."

"I will relieve you of them and have my lads start dissecting them come morning. By that smile on your face, I take it you think they will be useful to us."

"If the Secret Intelligence Service considers the names, various aliases and addresses of all the actual German spies currently operating in England, then yes. I do believe they will be useful."

The Colonel let out a low whistle. "Good work, sir. All we have had to date is reports from a mob of amateur sleuths who, thanks to a spate of absurd spy novels and the popular press, now imagine that every grocer selling sauerkraut is a German spy. Would that we had a network inside Germany. Almost everything we learn about them comes from Amsterdam, Geneva or St. Petersburg. We're going to have to move quickly to catch up on them. Your fine work is an excellent example of what can be done with some imagination and a bloody lot of patience. You've earned a good night's rest. Where are you staying?"

"We have rooms at Claridge's."

"Brilliant. We'll meet you there tomorrow morning at eight."

"Tomorrow, sir? You may have me mixed up with another one of your foot soldiers. This was the last role I agreed to play. Tomorrow, I shall return to my bees and my serene life on the Sussex Downs."

"My dear Mr. Holmes, I fear it is you who are mixed up. You have far too much valuable knowledge in your head for the SIS to allow you to be turned over to some queen bee in Sussex quite yet. Claridge's at eight. Good night, gentlemen."

He took the valise full of Von Bork's papers and vanished into the darkened building, leaving the two men alone on the pavement in the middle of a silent summer night.

"Holmes, what is he talking about?" asked Watson. "You've done your duty. What does he want you to do now?"

"I have not the foggiest idea, my friend. Most likely just a thorough accounting. The military are rather fond of facts and details."

As the car belonged to the SIS, they left it in a lane behind Whitehall and walked slowly back up to Mayfair. It was early August and the weather was mild. A gentle breeze caressed their faces as they talked about the adventures, fearful and joyful, that they had shared when they were both much younger men. At three o'clock in the morning of 3 August, the night guard opened the door of Claridge's, and they trudged up to their rooms.

Chapter Two

The Guilty Party

The Netherlands, 1891

e regret to inform you, Miss Zelle, but your time of training to be a teacher at our school has been terminated."

"But he was the one who started everything. It was he who made improper advances to me."

"Mr. Haanstra," said the head of the mothers' committee, "has had an unblemished reputation at this school, *his* school, for years before you came along. You used your exotic beauty to inflame his passions. Young women of your character do not belong molding the lives of our kindergarten children."

The headmaster of the school had found her attractive, indeed, rather irresistibly attractive. And she had to admit that she liked knowing that he wanted her. And she also had to admit that she thoroughly enjoyed their illicit times together.

However, now she was sixteen and, without a family to support her or any hope of finding respectable employment, Margaretha Zelle was on her own. If she had to find her own way in the world, she would. If her face was to be her fortune, so be it. If older men were beguiled by her olive complexion, dark hair, and tall, slender body, so much the better.

Her uncle took pity on her and brought her to live in The Hague. It was better than the provincial towns she had grown up in. The cafés, boulevards, music halls and shops entranced her, and she spent many hours admiring all the city had to offer. She visited the Mauritshuis and wondered who the kind and generous man had been that had given the beautiful young woman the pearl earring. Whilst using her meager allowance to enjoy a cup of coffee, she indulged in her favorite pastime—watching people, especially *those* people.

For The Hague was full of sailors and soldiers.

They were tanned and fit, with strong arms and chests, bleached hair and erect posture. The Netherlands maintained a substantial army and navy to service its overseas colonies in the Caribbean, South America, Africa and especially the Dutch East Indies. The Hague, a port city, was always teeming with handsome young men who had returned from duty in Sumatra, or Java, or Maluku.

She dreamed about them, but not about the young ones. She dreamed that a handsome captain of a naval vessel would come along and invite her to come aboard. She would accept and then would be off to enjoy the luxuries and the pleasures of the world. It was possible. Her model, her heroine, had done it.

Alone at night, she would read and reread the story of *the woman,* Irene Adler, in the copy of *The Adventures of Sherlock Holmes* her father had given her before he went bankrupt and abandoned his family.

Irene Adler was her ideal woman, beautiful and talented. She had enchanted a prince who was about to become a king. She was an adventuress and had had lovers and admirers from all over America and Europe. She was a famous singer and was called upon to perform in the great opera halls of the world. She had matched wits with the brilliant detective, Sherlock Holmes, and bested him. Soon, she would be married to a handsome and successful lawyer and would continue to live a life of privilege.

Margaretha would find a way to be like Irene Adler. She could sing well enough and had studied music, but she did not have the power to fill a hall with her voice. There would have to be another way.

One day that way appeared. As she was idly leafing through a newspaper, she noticed an advertisement in a lonely-hearts column. It read:

```
MARRIAGE
Captain in the East Indies currently on
leave seeks to return to the East Indies
as a married man. Seeking to meet a
cultured young lady of pleasant
appearance and gentle character. Any
fortune requisite. He will gladly meet
with parents or guardians to reach his
goal.
```

A lonely soldier. A captain. Why not take the chance? She answered the ad, enclosing a photograph of herself.

That was not a good idea.

Chapter Three

War is Declared

London, 3 August 1914

At half-past seven the next morning, Holmes and Watson sat in the breakfast room of Claridge's, enjoying a delectable full English. They continued to chat, as good friends do who have not seen each other for several years. Eventually, they got around to Von Bork, the documents, and the expected reporting session ahead.

"Any idea," asked Watson, "what all they will want to you to tell them about? You've been acquiring data in America and Ireland for over two years."

"I am blind as a mole as to where they will start, and it is a capital mistake to form a hypothesis —"

"Yes, for pity's sake, you've said that a thousand times. I know it is premature, but you must be wondering yourself, are you not?"

"Of course, I am. I suspect they will ask for my insights on the likelihood of America joining us should we be compelled to enter a war against Germany."

Watson put down his cup of coffee. "Well, will they?"

"No. For two reasons. First, the entire country and especially President Wilson are determined to keep out of European conflicts in which they have no significant interest. Hearst and Bryant are supporting that position. Second, all of their major cities are choc-a-block with Germans or the sons and daughters of Germans. They have money and they vote."

"And I assume," said Watson, "you have data on all the German organizations who are sending information and aid regularly to Kaiser Billy?"

"I do, and the sooner I can rid myself of it and return to my pleasant retreat on the Sussex Downs, the happier I'll be."

Watson grunted his approval, and the two of them returned to their coffee. On the dot of eight o'clock, another nondescript gray man in a gray suit entered the room and approached the table.

"Mr. Holmes and Doctor Watson, I presume?" he said.

"We are indeed," said Watson. "Would you like to join us for a coffee? The quality is excellent."

The gray man's face remained blank. "Thank you, doctor, but no. My instructions were to take you back to Whitehall Court for a meeting at twenty past eight. Kindly come with me now so we are not late."

"Good heavens," Watson sputtered into his coffee. "Why in the world are we being taken there? We can sit right here and chat as long as we don't talk too loudly."

"I'm sorry, Doctor, I am only following orders," he said, but with just a tiny flickering smile added, "There is a reason, sir, why it is called the Secret Service. Those of us who work

31

there just do our job and carry on and do not ask questions. Come, gentlemen, I have a car waiting."

They followed the man out of the hotel and onto Brook Street. A newsboy on the pavement was shouting at the top of his lungs. "WILL GERMANY DECLARE WAR ON FRANCE!? WILL FRANCE DECLARE WAR ON GERMANY!?"

The headline on the front of the *Daily Mail* he held under his arm asked the same questions.

Holmes bought a copy and, once inside the car, looked at the front page.

"I suspect that the answer is *yes*. Your thoughts, sir. Do you agree?" he said to the chap who had been sent to fetch them.

"With regret, sir, I cannot confirm anything. However, neither can I deny what you say. I suggest you ask Mr. Smith-Cumming when you meet with him."

"Merciful heavens," Watson said, "he's the top man at the SIS, is he not?"

"The grand panjandrum himself," said Holmes. "This should be interesting."

The car stopped at the same location they had been at during the night, and their escort led them to the same small door through which Von Bork had been carried.

"Good luck, gentlemen," said their driver. "It's been an honor to meet the two of you. Been a great fan of your stories. I expect you are about to be called on to do some sort of brave service to Great Britain. So, Godspeed, men."

Another gray man led them to the top floor and to a small waiting room. At precisely twenty minutes past eight, they were ushered into the office of Mr. Mansfield Smith-Cumming, the director of the foreign branch of Britain's intelligence services. He was dressed in a naval uniform, and the four stripes on his cuff identified him as a captain. He was reading a document as they entered and did not stand to greet them. With his left hand, he gestured to the two chairs facing his desk. As soon they were seated, he put down the document and looked directly at them.

"Good morning, gentlemen," he said. "Allow me to introduce myself."

"Not necessary and a waste of time," said Holmes, with more than a hint of arrogance. "You are Captain Mansfield George Smith-Cumming. Born in Lee. Over thirty years in the Royal Navy, mostly in command HMS Bellerophon. Your family is in banking and you married Leslie Marian Valiant-Cumming of County Moray and subsequently added the 'Cumming' name to yours, presumably because it had a more elevated ring to it than merely 'Smith.' In 1909 you were appointed to head up this new branch of government, although many were wondering why you were chosen. Is there any significant data you would like to add to your introduction, sir?"

The captain smiled and chuckled quietly. "Not a bit and your reputation is well-deserved, Mr. Holmes. Your exceptional store of knowledge is evident, as is your ability to recall it succinctly when necessary. Well done."

Then he laughed. "And if you thought you were going to protest that you were not qualified for whatever you are about to be asked to do, that demonstration of your singular abilities just undermined whatever argument you had rehearsed before you came in here. Jolly good of you, my man."

Smith-Cumming continued. "You did splendid work for us in America and down in Dover. Colonel Mountford told me that the files you obtained from the rascal Von Bork are worth their weight in gold. You will be in line for some sort of honor once these nasty days are over. But that is not important at the moment."

"I assume," said Holmes, "that you wish an extensive report on support for Germany in America."

"Perhaps in a week or two after you return."

"Return?" said Holmes, and he gave the director a sideways glance.

"So glad you asked, Mr. Holmes. Allow me to explain. Two days ago, the Kaiser declared war on his cousin, the Czar. By the end of this afternoon, we expect that he will declare war on France. We need to know in quite specific terms what he plans to do next. We sent him an ultimatum telling him not to advance into Belgium or such a move, in violation of Belgium's neutrality, would be casus belli. We know that France is moving her troops up to the frontier and is determined to regain possession of Alsace and Lorraine. If all that is going to happen is the two of them fight over a couple of border provinces, Britain has little at stake. We'll send the fleet to blockade the German ports and starve them out, but the risk to us will be low."

"These matters are hardly secret," said Holmes. "I fail to see what that has to do with me."

"I'm getting to that. You see, the *boche* may have more ambitious plans, the consequences of which to the Empire could be enormous."

"Surely, you know what their plans are, don't you?"

"Frankly, no, we don't. Of course, we've heard vaguely about Schlieffen's plan ever since he concocted it almost ten years ago. Paris for lunch, St. Petersburg for dinner was what it called for. But it has been revised numerous times since then, and we do not have the latest version of it. So, that, Mr. Holmes, is why you are here. You are going to find it for us."

"What do you need to know that you do not already? Von Moltke is going to invade France first and then Russia. Everyone already knows that."

"We need much more up-to-date data. What are von Moltke's latest and most specific plans? Where, precisely, is he going to send his army and how many men and artillery pieces? We need you to get over to the Continent, penetrate the German intelligence network and find that out. The future of Europe and the British Empire depends on it."

"You want to send me as a spy? With respect, sir, have you taken leave of your senses? I am now sixty years of age. I am a gray-haired older gentleman. I no longer have the physical stamina I had even a decade ago, and it is time I was put out to pasture."

"Ah, Mr. Holmes, it was reported to me that you man-handled Von Bork quite firmly. You survived a winter in Buffalo. Just because there is some snow beginning to appear on the rooftop, it does not mean there is no fire in the furnace. Your assignment will only be for a month, maybe two at most."

"I am flattered by your words. However, I have a realistic knowledge of the singular skills and abilities with which providence has endowed me, and I assure you, an understanding of a nation's military strategy is not amongst them. I have never served in the military and have little or no knowledge of military operations, let alone the expertise required for an analysis of plans for a large-scale war. You would be better off finding a younger man, one who has been trained at Sandhurst and has had battlefield experience. I have no doubt there are several within your ranks who meet those criteria."

"Your modesty, sir, is admirable but misplaced," said the director, "May I present a hypothetical problem? I understand you are quite the expert on analyzing them."

Holmes lowered his gaze and raised one eyebrow. "Proceed, sir."

"Let us say that I have a problem to solve. I need a report on, say, gold deposits in Rhodesia. I have two men to consider for the task. One is a brilliant and experienced mining engineer who has never been there. The other is a chap who was thoroughly familiar with the local people and customs but knows nothing about mining. Tell me, Mr. Holmes, if you were in my position, whom would you choose? Your answer, Mr. Holmes?"

Holmes paused before answering. "Clearly, it is much easier and quicker to teach an engineer about local customs than it is to teach expertise in mining engineering to a blank slate."

"Exactly. Now then, I am not looking for an up-and-coming major general. I need a man who has instincts for loyalty or betrayal. I need a man who can be imaginative and devious when his life and mission are in danger. I need a man who can see an ocean of data and clues and discern which are important and which are useless to him. In short, I need a spy."

Holmes exhaled a short sigh of exasperation. "Is there really not a younger man amongst your ranks who could do all that for you?"

"No."

"A Frenchman?"

"Please, Mr. Holmes. Be serious."

"Where are you trying to send me?"

"To Paris. You have been there several times and done excellent work, for which you were appropriately recognized."

"And should I refuse?"

"Terribly sorry, Mr. Holmes, but we are not giving you that option. We are conscripting you."

"Nonsense. There is no conscription in England, and even if there were, men my age are exempt."

"In your case, your singular case, sir, we shall make an exception. Welcome to His Majesty's Secret Service."

Holmes was silent for several seconds. Then he stood up and walked out of the room, leaving Watson alone with the somewhat confused director.

"What the …" muttered the director. "What is he doing?"

"Puffing on his pipe," said Watson. "I would guess that he considers this a two-pipe problem. Do relax. He'll be back. Allow me to suggest that you carry on with your paperwork until he returns."

Having said that, Dr. Watson took out his notebook and pencil and began to write. The director, after a minute of stunned silence, opened a file and read. Ten minutes later, Holmes returned.

"It appears I shall have to accept and will serve for as long as I am needed. However, I have two conditions. No, make that three."

"State them."

"Dr. Watson must be allowed to come with me."

"Oh, is that all? We have already assigned him. His kit has been assembled along with yours. We knew you would have to have someone to attend to you when you were shot or stabbed or tortured. Everything you need is waiting for you downstairs."

"Second. I will brook no interference in what I do and how I choose to do it. Not from anyone in France, and not even from you. Is that understood?"

The director laughed. "My dear, Mr. Holmes, we have all read the stories about you. We assumed, verily, we knew the way you work. You have carte blanche. What is your final condition?"

Holmes removed a small piece of paper from his pocket.

"I shall recruit an exceptionally capable accomplice in Paris. Your office will send a message immediately to the Ritz Hotel, requesting a meeting this evening. If we make haste, we should be in Paris in time for a late evening rendezvous. Say, eleven fifteen."

"We can do that. What's the chap's name?"

Holmes handed him the piece of paper. The director took it and then his eyes went wide.

"MATA HARI? Good lord, man, you cannot be serious. Why that woman has the most scandalous name in Europe since Catherine de Medici. She's danced naked in front of half the senior military and government men from Calais to Constanza, and she's been paid to visit the bedrooms of the other half."

"Precisely."

"Come now, sir. We may be spies, but we do have some standards to maintain."

"Do you? May I present a hypothetical problem to you? I understand you are quite the expert on analyzing them. If I had to choose between a morally impeccable diplomat and—"

"All right, all right. Your point is made. I'll have a wire sent off to the Ritz."

"Oh, one more thing," said Holmes.

"Yes, what is it."

"The English pound may be a sound currency, but it will be insufficient for use throughout Europe if war breaks out. I will need gold."

"Well, of course you will. There is a small pile with your kit. If you need more, we have an arrangement with the Rothschilds' bank, and you may pick up more at any branch."

Holmes stood and Watson joined him "Very well. When do we leave?"

"Pick up your kit and get yourself down to Dover in time for an evening crossing. And Mr. Holmes…"

"Yes?"

"Good luck and Godspeed."

Chapter Four

Becoming Mata Hari

The Hague, Netherlands, Spring 1895

Margaretha's letter with her photo was one of sixteen replies received by Captain Rudolf to his advertisement, seeking a wife. Maybe it was her photo, making her look enticing. Maybe it was what she wrote in the letter. She would never know, but he asked to meet her. So, on 24 March 1895, she went to the Rijksmuseum in Amsterdam and met him.

He was twenty years older than her but fit and energetic and wonderfully handsome in his captain's uniform. She found him attractive. He found her irresistible. The two of them entered into a passionate romance, culminating with their marriage and honeymoon in July 1895.

Her life was not luxurious but passably happy and satisfying, and her son, Norman, arrived in January 1897.

That period of her life was not to last. In May of that same year, her husband came to her.

"You need to pack," he told her. "My leave from the army is over. I have to return to my posting."

"Where are we going?" she asked.

"To the East Indies."

"To Batavia? Splendid. I hear it is the Queen of the Orient."

"We will spend some time there. Most of the time, I will be posted to smaller cities. You will like it. The Dutch people there are very welcoming."

Either he was foolishly wrong, or he lied to her.

Margaretha had a free, flirtatious spirit and did not fit in with the strait-laced Dutch colonists. Her dark, olive-skinned complexion led to gossip and rumors of her being part native. The colonists were highly bigoted and they would have nothing to do with her.

Rudolph returned to his habits of drinking far too much, gambling and not paying debts, and spending far too much time with his mistresses and in brothels. Margaretha was verbally abused and beaten. He blamed her for his not getting promoted.

"My life here is not what I had hoped for," she wrote in a letter to a friend back in Holland. "But I have found two activities that have made it tolerable. I had learned to ride horses when I was a child. Here, I have become an expert. I ride at least twice a week and *Princess,* my favorite mare, and I have become good friends. When I am galloping on top of her, the thrill and exhilaration is sublime."

As she was not able to make friends amongst the other European women, she became close to the native women of the various towns in which her husband was posted. She loved to watch their sensuous moves and graceful twirls as they performed their traditional dances. They taught her how to dance like they did.

"For these women," she wrote in another letter, "dancing is not merely a form of amusement. It is sacred, an act of worship. I have worked hard at learning how to dance like they do. Last week I was

40

overjoyed when my instructor told me that the women of the village had bestowed a new name on me. From here on, I was to be known as *the eye of the dawn.* That's what it means in my language, but in the language they speak here, my name is *Mata Hari.*"

Her daughter Jeanne was born in the East Indies, but her marriage continued to deteriorate. Her children got sick and her son died. She separated from Captain MacLeod, then got back together with him. They returned to the Netherlands in 1902 and formally separated with the legal agreement that he would pay support to her and her daughter. He never did, but he did take their daughter away from her.

With no husband, no income, and not the type of reputation that would allow her to be a school teacher or governess, she did what any sensible, single woman would do in Europe in 1903.

She moved to Paris.

Putting her equestrian skills to work, she first found work riding horses in a circus. That did not last long. Then she tried something that would change her life, and history. She performed an exotic, erotic dance.

At first, her dances were for private audiences. Then she performed at the *Musée National des Arts Asiatiques* where she was embraced by both critics and the museum's founder, M. Émile Étienne Guimet. After that, there was no stopping her. She danced in night clubs, with ballet ensembles and in solo performances in the great opera houses of Europe. She was the talk-of-the-town in every capital of Europe and beloved by the avant-garde of the fin de siècle. Princes, aristocrats, captains of industry and military leaders all enjoyed her company and showered her with furs, jewelry, hotel suites and cash.

It couldn't last. It didn't last. Soon the competition emerged. Isadora Duncan was a brilliant, trained dancer. Maud Allan was a Canadian pianist turned exotic dancer and stunningly beautiful. But there was something they did not have. They were not exotic princesses. She was. Her new persona became:

41

Born in Java, in the midst of tropical vegetation, I have been taught from my earliest childhood the deep meaning of these dances which constitute a cult, a religion. Only those born and bred there become impregnated with their religious significance, and can impart to them that solemn note to which they can lay claim.

The fact that the story of her origin was fictitious didn't bother her, and the press repeated it endlessly. Along the way, *Margaretha* faded away, and she became *Mata Hari.*

After a decade of fame, her star began to fade. Her body aged and softened. Younger, prettier women who were better dancers competed with her. The invitations to perform came less and less often. She now did what any sensible, single woman would do in Europe in 1913.

She became a courtesan to an endless stable of wealthy, powerful men, especially generals and colonels.

During the first week of August 1914, she received a message telling her that a famous Englishman wished to meet her but was not interested in any form of intimacy. He wanted to make use of her still impressive singular skills and intelligence. She recognized his name. He was the man the stories of whose adventures had introduced her to Irene Adler, her hero. She agreed to meet him on 4 August in the bar of the Hotel Ritz on the Place Vendôme.

Chapter Five

The Ferry to Calais

3 August, 1914

Two hours after their meeting in Whitehall, Holmes and Watson boarded a Southeastern train at Victoria. For much of the journey down to Dover, they napped. On arriving, they hurried to catch an afternoon ferry to France.

In the middle of the summer, a Channel crossing is a pleasant experience. As the traveler departs the docks of Dover, the white cliffs fade behind him, and the sun descends to the western horizon. Soon, the lights on the hills behind Calais will emerge. On a good crossing, the breeze is warm and the sea calm. The ferry will rock ever so gently.

On normal days during those years before 1914, the boat was full of both English and French men of commerce and their wives or mistresses coming and going to the business offices and warehouses of their respective countries. In early August, it was also packed with American tourists either having done Paris or on their way to do it.

The third of August was not a normal day.

The ferry that arrived from France had been packed to overflowing. The return run back to Calais was nearly empty. Talk of war had reduced those wanting to visit France to a handful. Holmes and Watson had the boat almost to themselves, and they proceeded directly to the open deck at the prow where passengers could stand and gaze across the water,

"Watson," said Holmes, "did you by chance happen to notice the fellow who was not far behind us in the queue? He was wearing a hat and a rather stylish long gabardine coat with a waist belt?"

"I did. Quite the sharp dresser, I must say. A lovely new Aquascutum. They are quite the rage amongst our army officers, well, those with money. I fancy getting one for myself, or do you think I am too old for such an indulgence?

"He's following us."

"Holmes, all he did was get on to the same ferry. So did a dozen others. What makes you suspicious of him? Or do you suspect him because he is dressed too smartly for your taste?"

"He got on the same train as we did at Victoria."

"As does everyone who ever goes from London to France," said Watson. "That's where the trains to Dover leave from."

"He has been casting furtive glances at us a few times too often."

"Fine. If he is still tagging along behind us after we get to France, I shall start to be worried. Until then, do try to enjoy the voyage. It's likely to be our last opportunity to relax for several weeks."

Holmes lit his pipe, and the two of them did indeed attempt to relax until the rocking of the boat and the vibrations of the engines had the effect on their bodies that is universal to the male of the species beyond the age of fifty.

"If you will excuse me," said Holmes, "I shall pay a visit to the lavatory."

"I'm coming with you," said Watson.

The two of them made their way down the steep ship's staircase and into the lavatory. As they were standing, facing the wall, the door opened behind them.

"Herr Holmes and Doktor Watson?" said the man who had entered the room.

The two of them hastily adjusted themselves and turned to face the man in the crisp new Aquascutum overcoat. He took a Luger P08 pistol from his pocket and aimed it directly at the center of Holmes's chest.

Watson instinctively slipped his hand into his pocket and felt for his service revolver.

"We are," said Holmes, "and who might you be?"

"*Es tut nichts zur Sache.* Your foul deeds last night in Dover greatly inconvenienced our work. You cannot proceed to France to do any more damage."

"Oh, is that all that is bothering you?" said Holmes. "Very well then, you can watch over us and make sure we go back to England on the return run. Will that do?"

"*Nein*, you have to die now."

"How are you going to explain our bodies in the lavatory? There are so few people on board, everyone will know it was you who shot us."

"I shall throw you overboard," said the assailant.

"That won't do," said Holmes. "I assure you, Dr. Watson and I are strong swimmers. We could likely make it back to shore and return on the next ferry."

"Don't be *dumm.* You will be dead. Dead men cannot swim."

He fixed his aim, and the sound of two shots exploded in the close confines of the gentlemen's lavatory. Watson closed his eyes, expecting to feel one of them drilling through his breast, and he said a quick prayer commending his soul to its maker.

He felt nothing. When he opened his eyes, he saw Holmes standing beside him and the chap who had been pointing a gun at him prone on the floor. There were two distinct holes in the back of his coat.

"Merciful heavens, Holmes. What happened?"

The door of one of the toilet stalls opened.

"I believe I happened, Doctor Watson," said the sturdily built chap who had been in the stall. He was wearing the uniform of a Lieutenant in the Royal Navy and was also holding a Luger.

"Terribly sorry," he said, "that you had such an unpleasant start to your mission. My superiors suspected that there is a spy in Cumming's office, and I was assigned to shadow you in case you were impeded."

"Was it necessary," said Holmes, "to kill him?"

"I wish it hadn't been. We could have put his arse in a wringer and squeezed all kinds of intelligence out of him. But had I only wounded him, he could still have got a shot off, and you would be dead, sir. We can't take that chance. Your mission is far too important."

"Pray tell," said Holmes. "Who is the 'we' that assigned you to follow us?"

"Again, terribly sorry, sir. But I cannot divulge that information. Everything has gone secret now that war is in the offing."

"Can you at least tell us to whom we should be grateful for saving our lives?

"You mean me, Mr. Holmes? Aye, I can tell you that. My name's O'Hara. Steven O'Hara. But don't waste your time asking about me. You will not find me in any register of His Majesty's Armed Forces. Officially, I don't exist."

He had put his pistol back in a holster under his jacket and leaned down to the corpse on the floor. He grabbed the collar of the coat and dragged him toward the door.

"Would you mind, Doctor," he said, "holding the door open. I have to dispose of this *boche* before anyone else has to use the facilities."

Watson held the door open. "What are you going to do with him?" he asked.

"Toss him overboard. It will be a week before his superiors conclude that he's vanished. And thcy will attribute his demise to Sherlock Holmes. You reputation, sir, precedes you."

Once the lieutenant had departed, dragging the would-be killer behind him, Watson turned to Holmes.

"Shame about the coat," said Watson. "He was my size. Why couldn't he have shot him in the head?"

"Awfully bloody," said Holmes. "Far too much mess to clean up."

"So, who is he working for if not Smith-Cumming?"

"I haven't the foggiest," said Holmes. "By his accent, he's a Yorkshire tyke, and you know what the rest of England says about them."

"No. What?"

"Shake a bridle over a Yorkshireman's grave, and he'll rise from the dead and steal your horse."

"Ah, so you don't trust him? Even after he saved our lives?"

"The world, my dear Doctor, is going to war. I suggest that we do not trust anyone completely."

Chapter Six

Arriving in Paris

o one followed them off the boat, but the assembled mob who were trying to board the ferry back to England were pushing and shoving and shouting.

They hurried to the Calais train station in time to catch the evening train to Paris.

At the Calais station, they learned what had taken place while they were crossing the Channel. Newsboys were shouting, *La France déclare la guerre*! France and Germany had declared war on each other.

The train, like the ferry they had come on, was almost empty. No one was on their way to Paris.

Twilight, *l'heure bleue,* had fallen as they passed through the fields of Picardie and south toward Paris. At ten o'clock that evening, the train slowed and pulled into the station.

The Gare du Nord was in utter chaos. It was pouring rain. Several thousand people were trying to board any train that would take them away from Paris and out of France. Families with weary, crying children and babes in arms were struggling with their few suitcases to find the train cars to which they had been assigned. Elderly men and women were getting wheeled through the mob in bath chairs by their sons and daughters, all looking distraught. Holmes and Watson passed a guy standing on a station platform in the rain, with a comical look on his face. He was reading a note and looked as if his insides had been kicked out.

They edged and elbowed their way against the tide of humanity until they reached the line of Renault taxis standing on the street that ran along the west side of the station. The driver smiled as they approached. He looked as if he had been waiting for a long time for anyone who wanted to be driven into the heart of the city.

"Hotel Ritz," Holmes told the driver. *"Premier arrondissement."*

"Bienvenue à Paris," replied the driver. *"Mais vous êtes anglais.* Why do you make a visit to Paris?"

"To enjoy the art and nightlife of the City of Light," said Holmes.

"Heh, êtes-vous fous? Can you not see? Everyone who can is running away to Calais, or Dieppe, or Le Havre. Any port that can take them out of France. We are at war."

"But your army," said Watson, "your *Grande Armée.* Surely, they will protect you from the Germans, will they not?"

"Peut-être. But they did not do so well the last time they fought the Germans. *Les vieux,* the old people, they remember. They remember the siege when everyone starved. There is very much fear in the city. *Bien sûr,* you have not come from England to have a good time. Are you bringing in rifles and ammunition? Perhaps you are taking your money out while you can. It is none of my affair, but I wish you *bonne chance."*

"You are a clever man," said Holmes. "I confess, we have come to rescue my sister and help her return to London."

"You sister? *Sans vouloir vous offenser, m'sieur.* But if your sister is living at the Ritz, then she is either a spy or one of the *grandes horizontales.* These are the only customers now of the Ritz. All the American tourists and English *hommes d'affaires* have departed."

"But you," said Watson. "You are still here. Are you not worried?"

"*Moi?* No. I am only a driver of a taxi, one of thousands in this city. It does not matter who is in control, they will always need us to take them places. If they kill us, they will have to walk. If the war comes all the way to Paris, they will need us to move all those *gros cul* generals from one front to the other. *Bien sûr*, we will be here forever. So, whenever you need a taxi, you have them call for Mathieu Leboeuf, and I will make for you a good drive. *À la prochaine fois, mes amis.*"

Except for taxis that were taking Parisiens to the Gare du Nord or Gare de l'Est, the streets were clear of traffic, and they soon arrived at the Hotel Ritz in the Place Vendôme. The opulent lobby was quiet, although they could hear a low chatter coming from the bar. The brass-buttoned and epauletted young man behind the front desk welcomed them in English and French, and a similarly uniformed bellhop carried their bags up to their rooms. At eleven o'clock on the evening of 2 August they entered the bar and were escorted to a table.

About a third of the tables were occupied and no one was speaking loudly. As they sat in silence, they mostly heard French being spoken, with a few words of English here and there and one lone table of men chattering in Spanish. Four glamorous young women each sat at a table across from a well-dressed man, and two more sat at the bar. All were sipping on glasses of what appeared to be champagne.

"This woman," said Holmes, "is supposed to meet us at a quarter past eleven. She is reputed to have been born and raised in

Java and therefore, if she is like all the other men and women I have met from that part of the world, she is quite likely to be late."

She wasn't.

At precisely fifteen minutes past eleven, the woman who had been born Margaretha Zelle but was now known throughout Europe as Mata Hari entered the bar of the Ritz. Holmes and Watson looked at her as she stood for a moment in the entrance and glanced around the room. Her gaze settled on the two of them, and she walked purposefully but not quickly toward them. The eyes of most of the men in the room, even those who had been chatting with a woman, followed her.

It was impossible not to notice her. She was tall. With the help of the heels on her black patent leather boots, she was at least six feet in stature. Except for a white blouse that did little to cover her cleavage, she was dressed entirely in black. Her short jacket had padded shoulders and was secured by one button at the approximate height of her navel. Her skirt was tight, extending to her calves and cut up the side to facilitate her long stride. The part of it that tightly covered her hips and backside looked as if it could have been applied with a paintbrush. Her hat was wide-brimmed and sloped to one side of her head.

She looked directly at Holmes and Watson as she approached their table. They could not help staring back at her dark eyes, hair and eyebrows and her olive complexion. They stood to greet her. She was as tall as Holmes and lowered her gaze three inches to smile at Watson.

"Mr. Sherlock Holmes and Dr. Watson, I presume," she said, speaking English with a faint hint of a Dutch accent. As soon as they were seated, she gave Holmes a long, intense look.

"Forgive my staring at you, Mr. Holmes, but you remind me so much of the fifth man who proposed marriage to me this year."

"Do I indeed? And just how many proposals have you received?"

"Four."

51

Holmes was momentarily nonplussed, and the woman burst out laughing, and smiled at him. "Well, Mr. Holmes, I am terribly attracted to men with superior minds, and I do believe that you are the cleverest man in this room. Would you not agree?" She laughed again and touched Holmes's forearm ever so slightly.

"As we have only just arrived," said Holmes, "I am not in a position to judge the other men who are here."

"Oh, then let me help you," she said. "All you have to do is observe them closely. The best-dressed and best-looking ones are all spies. You can tell by the way they speak French. Their accents are all too perfectly Parisian, and they are drinking expensive champagne. The ones in the cheap suits who are still sipping their first drink are reporters, mainly from England and America."

"They must be well-paid," said Watson, "if they can afford to stay in this hotel."

She laughed again. "Oh, my dear Doctor, they do not stay here. They share rooms in shabby hotels in the *Quartier Latin* and come to this bar and pretend to be important. Before all the German men vanished last week, they kept asking them questions about what the Kaiser was going to do next and, of course, the Germans told them lies. Some of those Germans were quite amusing. Pity that they have all gone."

"The French men would be happy to see them depart," said Holmes, "given that they are now at war."

"*Mais oui*, the Frenchmen, the ones who have not yet fled, are deputy cabinet ministers or owners of industries. They're not worried about the war. They will always be well-paid by whoever is in charge of the country. So there, Mr. Holmes. You see. You have a better brain than any of them. What else would you like to know?"

"Thank you, madam, for so enlightening me. I assure you, I have no interest in reporting a story to the English press, nor of conducting business. I believe you know why we are here."

"Yes, of course, I do. But I simply cannot carry on a conversation with such an intelligent man without something to help my mind function."

She waved her bejewelled hand, and a waiter appeared at the table in five seconds.

"*Oui, madam? Champagne? Comme d'habitude?*"

"Yes, Pierre. These fine gentlemen would like a bottle of your finest champagne."

"But, of course, madam."

The waiter waved his hand, and another man, a younger one, appeared at the table carrying a magnum of a select brand and three fluted glasses. He poured them, tilting the bottle and glasses ever so expertly, allowing them to fill to the brim without the foam overflowing.

"To our success," she said, lifting her flute. She slowly swallowed the entire glass, and the attentive waiter poured her another.

"To success," said Holmes and took a minuscule sip. He then set his glass down. "Now, madam, to business, please."

"Why, of course. But one question first, if I may?"

"Certainly."

"Do tell me, Mr. Holmes, how is Irene Adler? Have you heard from her recently? Is she still the wonderful adventuress as she approaches sixty that she was when she was thirty? I must tell you, sir, *the woman* has been my hero since I was a child."

Holmes was not expecting that question but nodded and replied. "I regret that Miss Adler, of dubious and questionable memory, has not kept in contact with me."

"What a pity. I was hoping that someday I might meet her. Oh well, I suppose we can move on to less important matters. What is it you want from me?"

Chapter Seven

Meeting Mata Hari

"**Y**ou are Dutch, yes? And you have a Dutch passport?" asked Holmes.

"I do. The Netherlands is a neutral country. I am not at war with anyone. I can travel anywhere I want."

"Are you willing to do some work on behalf of England?"

"I will work for whoever pays me well."

"Even if the work is dangerous?"

"Mr. Holmes, what could be more dangerous than dancing in front of three thousand of the richest members of Paris society and progressively removing my seven veils? I was sure that someone would murder me the following day, but here I am. Knowing that one's life is in danger is utterly intoxicating. Being paid whilst living that way is even better."

"Excellent. I am told that you are on friendly terms with several of the most powerful German generals. Is that correct?"

"Ah, so you want me to meet a general … and what? Extract information from him? You want me to be a spy for England?"

"Yes."

"What do you want me to get, and what will you pay me?"

"A copy of the most current German plans for the invasion of France, and you will be paid the equivalent of five hundred British pounds … in gold, of course."

She took a long, slow sip of her champagne. "I would be quite happy to accept your offer, sir, but what you ask may be impossible, even for me."

"And why is that?" asked Holmes.

"Only the highest-ranked German generals will have seen those plans. None of them will be easy to meet with. Karl von Bulow is with his army on the border of Belgium and starting to cross over. No civilian who is not German can get anywhere close to him. Remus von Woyrsch has been sent to the east. He is several hundred miles away. Von Bothmer is fighting the Russians. I suppose that does not make much difference since all of them are over sixty years old and their interest in a beautiful woman is, shall we say, *flagging*?"

"Then who is on the western front and still susceptible to your charms?"

"Generals Falkenhayn and Hindenberg are both my good friends, but they are also living at the border of Belgium, and I cannot get through to them. The last I heard, Erich Ludendorff is in Berlin. It would take me several days to get there. Maybe longer now that the German railroads have been commandeered by the army to move their men. Admiral Scheer will be on his battleship up in Wilhelmshaven."

"Fine. Who else is there?"

"There are several generals with lower ranks, but they would not likely have the information you need. Let me think for a few minutes."

She finished her second glass of champagne and waved at the waiter to refill it. After another generous swallow, she looked over at Holmes and smiled.

"I do believe that it was you who said that when you eliminate the impossible, whatever remains must be the truth. Yes? The one who remains is Johann von Bernstorff. He will do splendidly."

"But he's in Washington. He's the Ambassador to America," said Holmes.

"That is the father. I am speaking of the son. He is the Ambassador to the Netherlands. I have met him several times in Amsterdam. He is exceptionally knowledgeable and a favorite of the Kaiser."

"Ah, yes," said Holmes. "I have heard of this man. He is reputed to be brilliant and very difficult to deal with."

"My dear, Mr. Holmes," she said. "He is a man. Like all men, when they are drunk and in the throes of ecstasy, he will be easy."

"That may well be. But I must warn you, he has a reputation amongst men who have encountered him of being dangerous."

She laughed. "And a reputation amongst women of falling asleep immediately after, if you know what I mean."

Sherlock Holmes blushed ever so slightly. "Very well then. We shall accompany you to Amsterdam and expect that you will deliver the data on the current battle plans within twenty-four hours. Can you do that?

"Perhaps. It all depends on what you are willing to pay, Mr. Holmes."

He reached into his pocket and extracted a handful of gold coins. Having placed them on the table, he slid them over to her. Without inspecting them, she placed them in her purse.

"Oh, you do know how to make a lady happy, don't you?"

She stood up from her chair in the bar at the Ritz Hotel in Paris. "I do believe I shall enjoy working with you, Mr. Holmes."

Without warning, she bent down and planted a kiss on the cheek of Sherlock Holmes and then stood back up and gave him an odd look.

"*Mon dieu,* why is it I feel nothing from you? Were you neutered as a schoolboy?"

"Madam, a man must choose between being susceptible to the wiles of a woman, or being a good detective. He cannot be both. Tomorrow morning at six?"

"An utterly ungodly hour, but yes. Tomorrow at the door at six."

The woman known to the world as Mata Hari turned and glided her way out of the bar. The eyes of every man in the room followed her.

Chapter Eight

Seduction in Amsterdam

At ten minutes before six o'clock, Holmes and Watson descended to the lobby of the hotel, where Watson procured an English-language newspaper from the front desk. He read the headlines and hurried over to Holmes's side.

"Holmes, look. It says that Asquith and Grey sent a message to Germany demanding that they honor Belgium's neutrality. If the Germans invade, it will be cause for war between us and the Germans."

Holmes read the headline and brief story that accompanied it. "It would be best, then, if we get across Belgium and back as quickly as possible."

"You don't believe the Germans will retreat?"

"Their Chancellor, Herr Bethmann Hollweg, dismissed the Treaty of London, guaranteeing Belgium's neutrality, as a mere scrap of paper. I expect that they will think they are calling our bluff and ignore the threat of war."

"And then invade?"

"If Belgium does not give them permission, which up until now they have refused to do, then yes."

"And then we will declare war?"

"Precisely. Therefore, time is of the essence."

To her credit, Mata Hari appeared at exactly six o'clock, transported by a taxi and accompanied by several pieces of luggage.

"I am impressed, madam," said Watson, "with your punctuality. Well done."

She shrugged. "I am the best in Europe at what I do. And what I do requires that the men who are paying me are not kept waiting. It is good for business."

"Excellent," said Holmes. "We must make haste to the Gare du Nord and obtain our tickets if we wish to be in Amsterdam by this evening."

"Not necessary," said Mata Hari. "I already have them. We will need to change trains in Lille and Antwerp, but we have first-class cabins to ourselves all the way to Amsterdam."

"Can we not travel through Brussels?" asked Watson. "It would be much quicker, would it not?"

"By the time we get there, the Germans will be advancing on it. Our only route is across the north of the county."

"Ah, yes," said Watson. "Well done, my dear. You have traveled this route before, I assume."

Again, she shrugged. "For the past ten years I have traveled to every capital city in Europe. It is not difficult. Come, and please pay the driver well. As a favor to me, he has postponed trying to get his family out of Paris."

The Gare du Nord was still in chaos as French citizens jostled their way onto trains that would take them to the Channel ports. Fortunately, no one was interested in taking the train to Lille and up to the border with Belgium. The three of them caught the first train of the morning and chugged quietly and peacefully north into Picardy, across the River Somme and into Flanders. The gently undulating fields brimming with waving wheat, meandering sheep, and poppies in full display were a universe away from the armies massing a hundred miles to the south and the apocalyptic events that were about to descend on humankind.

They changed trains in Lille and crossed the border into Belgium. From there they journeyed to the northeast through Ghent and on to Antwerp. Although they were ensconced in their own cabin, all the conversations they overheard when the train stopped at the stations along the way were muted, and full of fear. It seemed as if the entire world was hoping and praying that war would be averted at the last minute, yet knowing that it would not.

Antwerp was far enough to the north of the regions where the Germans had massed their armies that the people acted as if they would be spared. And so they were, for a while.

Once they crossed into Holland and stopped briefly in Breda, the mood of the populace had changed from night to day. The Netherlands was a neutral country, and the preferences of the Dutch were divided between the French and the Germans. The queen, Wilhelmina, was known to be partial to the French and English, although her husband, Duke Henry, was himself a German and a thoroughgoing devotee of all things German. He was particularly enamored of the German army and German mistresses. The gossip of the day was unequivocal in noting that the duke and the queen did not get along.

By late in the afternoon on the fourth day of August, they arrived at the palatial Amsterdam Centraal Station. Hundreds of Dutch men and women were making their way toward the trains that were departing the central district of Amsterdam and would take them to their homes in the hinterland. The conversations were quiet and the faces glum. The shouts of the newsboys and the headlines of the newspapers conveyed the reason for the atmosphere of foreboding. Belgium had refused to allow the Kaiser's army to march across their nation, and Germany had declared war on Belgium. The German army was now advancing toward Liège.

"Holmes," said Watson, "are you certain that we are safe if we continue here in Holland? It's a neutral country as well, but that did not do much for poor little Belgium."

"Holland has an advantage. It would be far more difficult to advance into France through it than through Belgium. However, I suspect that our chances of obtaining the documents we are after and getting back to France through Belgium have diminished now that fighting has started. I expect that Mata Hari's friendly ambassador will be otherwise engaged. What say you, madam?"

"I sent a wire at midnight to my dear sweet Johann," said Mata Hari, "letting him know that I would be in the city and suggesting dinner this evening at eight at the Grand Hotel. I have not heard back, of course, but I am sure he will appear."

"Logic would suggest," said Holmes, "that he will be occupied around the clock with the affairs of state what with the declarations of war."

"My dear Mr. Holmes, Johann is not yet thirty-five years old. At that age, all men still think with their little heads, not their big ones. He will be there. Come, it is a short walk from the station to the Dam. I need to be at the hotel in time to prepare myself for the evening. Please wait for me in your rooms. I should have what you want in time for breakfast tomorrow."

Holmes and Watson entered the splendidly appointed dining room of the Grand Hotel at half-past seven. In the center of each of the tables was a large vase overflowing with dahlias and canna lilies. The conversations at the tables were hard to hear. No one was laughing. Europe had gone to war.

They requested a table near the back corner of the room from which they could see the other patrons. At ten minutes before eight o'clock, a tall, blond, impeccably dressed young man entered and was seated at a table near the door.

"Watch him carefully," said Holmes to Watson. "If he is the man he is reputed to be, there is something you will not see him do."

"What?"

"Touch his face with his fingers. It is the mark of a very controlled character. He will sit with his hands in his lap until she appears. He will not touch his ears, or scratch his face or fidget with the silverware."

Watson watched. His Excellency, Herr Johann von Bernstorff, the Ambassador of the Kaiser to Holland, serenely gazed around the room and then sat still, his eyes fixed on nothing as he appeared to be lost in thought. Then he glanced again over the other patrons.

"His hands have not moved," said Watson. "He certainly possesses a remarkable degree of self-control."

"Indeed he does," said Holmes. "He is known to be very German and to have a singularly brilliant mind."

"Do you believe your Mata Hari can get what she wants from him?"

"She is not *my* Mata Hari. She is not anybody's Mata Hari. She belongs to no one but herself. As to whether or not she will be successful, only time will tell."

At precisely eight o'clock, Mata Hari appeared at the entrance of the dining room. The maître d' escorted her to von Bernstorff's table, and the young man rose to his feet as she approached. With effortless grace, he accepted her hand, lifted it to his lips, and released it, smiling. She was dressed in a lavender gown that was sufficiently tight around the hips and deeply cut at the neckline to be stunning without crossing the line and into the realm of vulgar.

"My goodness," whispered Watson, "but she is a stunner. I dare say she will make enemies of every other woman in this room."

"Physical beauty, my friend," said Holmes, "is a divine gift that is appreciated by all to whom it has also been given and resented only by those to whom it has been refused. She will use her gifts skillfully to accomplish her goal. We shall not be waiting for long."

The young ambassador and his dinner companion enjoyed a glass of champagne and a plate of *foie gras* whilst chatting and smiling at each other. Her gaze never left his eyes, and on three occasions she reached her hand over and lightly touched his wrist. After half-an-hour and another two glasses of champagne, they rose and departed without ordering dinner.

"What do we do now?" asked Watson.

"We wait in our rooms until she reappears."

"Do you truly believe she will be able to coax the information you need out of him?"

"If she fails, we shall have to imagine an alternative plan. Until then, I am counting on her. She is a woman of singular and peerless talents."

After consuming a dinner of some favorite dish of the Dutch—with Holmes duly noting that 'Dutch cuisine' was a type of oxymoron—Holmes and Watson retired to their hotel rooms and waited.

At five o'clock on the morning of 5 August, Mata Hari tapped lightly on Dr. Watson's door. "I have it," she told him. "Kindly rouse Mr. Holmes and meet me at the front door of the hotel in thirty minutes. We need to get back to Paris whilst we still can."

Chapter Nine

Reviewing the Plan

At that hour on a Wednesday morning, there were no taxicabs available, and the three of them walked quickly up the Damrak from the hotel to the Centraal Station. A bellboy followed them, pushing a luggage cart along the cobblestones. Not wanting to have anything they said to each other overheard, they did not speak. Once they reached the station, Mata Hari strode to the ticket office.

"The trains are still running across the north of Belgium," she said. "They've stopped anything south of Brussels. I have tickets for us through to Lille. A cabin to ourselves. From there we can get back to Paris. We leave in twenty-five minutes. We have time for coffee, bread and cheese in the café."

Holmes picked up a newspaper from a boy who was shouting in Dutch.

"What is he saying?" he asked Mata Hari.

"Yesterday, President Wilson declared American neutrality. The Germans will be happy to hear that."

They gulped breakfast quickly and found the way to their cabin. Once inside, Holmes lit a cigarette and offered one to his female fellow traveler. She accepted. For a few minutes, the three of them sat in silence and enjoyed the deceptive sense of calm that tobacco imparts. Once the train was underway, Holmes asked the obvious question.

"Were you successful?"

"Entirely."

"Entirely, madam?"

From her handbag, she retrieved a thin, bound document and handed it to Holmes.

"The most recent revision of Herr Schlieffen's plan as modified a fortnight ago by Herr von Moltke. Do you need help translating it from the German?"

Holmes took the document from her and opened the cover. The title read *Aufmarsch III Westen,* and it bore the embossed indicia of the double-headed eagle of the Kaiser's realm. He leafed through the pages and nodded.

"Having worked with the Germans for two years in America, I can get by reading their guttural language. I shall seek your assistance if I need it. But I dare say, madam, well done. And I dare not ask how much and in what manner you paid him for this copy."

"Not a single centime. Not a bloody English farthing," she said, grinning broadly. "God's truth, Mr. Holmes, is that he paid me. Rather handsomely."

"I beg your pardon, madam?"

"Twenty thousand francs, to be exact, and I do believe I have found myself a lovely new source of income. Oh, but it means that you will have to make your own copy of that plan. I have to deliver it on behalf of dear Johann to a location in Paris. I suggest you start copying. If you do so diligently, you should be able to have it finished by the time we get to Paris."

Holmes's eyes went wide, and he stubbed out the remnants of his cigarette

"He paid you to deliver this plan to an agent in Paris?"

"That is what I said, sir. Enough to keep me in the style to which I have become accustomed for at least three months. All I have to do is deliver documents and information back and forth between Paris and Amsterdam. As a citizen of neutral Holland, I can do that."

"Madam! That makes you a spy, an agent of the enemy."

"*Ne sois pas absurd.* I will be an agent of nothing. Whatever I tell anyone will be no more than what any one of them could read in the newspapers. Of course, I shall let the boys in France know what I am doing, and I expect they will pay me as well or better."

"That strikes me," said Holmes, "as utterly shameless opportunism, completely devoid of any sense of honor whatsoever."

"Does it, sir? It strikes me as a jolly good way for a woman of my age who is alone in this world to survive and prosper whilst all those honorable men on all sides send much younger men to be slaughtered. Let me know if you need help with the translation."

She pulled a novel from her handbag, a copy of the recently published fantastical story, *The Poison Belt,* and settled back into her seat. She only lifted her eyes from her book when Holmes took out his cigarettes. Each time he did so, she cadged another one from him.

Holmes had taken out a pencil and a notebook and had focused his concentration on the German document. He was scribbling his translation as rapidly as he could, pausing every twenty minutes or so to light another cigarette. Before each short break, he made a small mark on the page he was translating to remind him where to start again.

They had changed trains in Lille and took the only train of the day going back to Paris, a milk run that would get them to the Gare du Nord by the late afternoon. They were rolling through Picardie when Holmes looked up at Watson.

"This plan … it is utterly devious, deceptive, completely unexpected by our side … it's … it's brilliant. If they implement it, then this war truly will be over by Christmas. The Germans will have won. They will have occupied France and will control the Channel ports."

"Indeed? How could they do that?"

"Their incursion into Belgium is a mere feint, a blind. It is intended to draw our BEF into the north of France and force the French troops to move north from attacking Alsace and up into Belgium. Whilst they are doing that, the Germans will move the bulk of their forces south all the way to the border of Switzerland and sweep into France from Basel. They will be completely unopposed, and then they will encircle our boys and the French from the south and west."

"Ah, so they will change from a right hook to an uppercut with their left."

"Precisely … and it terrifies me. We have to get this data back to Whitehall immediately."

"Hold on," said Mata Hari. "You can't take that document to England. I promised Johann I'd leave it at the desk of the Hotel du Louvre tonight. You have to let me fulfill my role if you want me to keep helping you."

"For whom are you leaving it?"

"A Mr. Smith, whoever he is."

"Quite acceptable, madam," said Holmes. "I have copied all the details we need. You may deliver the document to your Mr. Smith. We shall bid you *adieu* at the station and be on our way."

"Please, my dear Mr. Holmes, you cannot get a train to Calais until tomorrow morning. You may as well escort me to dinner. I do hate dining alone."

"If you insist."

"Oh, you are such a sweet man … even if neutered. The Ritz at nine."

Chapter Ten

It Cannot Be Done

olmes and Watson parted company with Mata Hari upon arriving in Paris, with a promise to meet again in the dining room of the Ritz.

"If you would be so kind, my friend," said Holmes, "please do whatever is necessary and spend however much is needed to book our tickets tomorrow morning on the train back to Calais. I shall find a cup of tea in the station café and review my translation of General Schlieffen's more than somewhat revised plan. Take a few gold coins and disperse them liberally."

While Watson bought first-class tickets to Calais for the full price, augmented by a generous bribe or two, Holmes made edits and improvements to the information he would convey to the government of Great Britain the following day. He had been at it for a half-an-hour when Watson returned, grinning triumphantly.

"Done. A private cabin on the first train. Who says that French officials are arrogant and unfriendly? You should have seen the smiles when I dropped the gold in front of them. They—"

"Watson! Enough."

"Merciful heavens. What's wrong now. I thought you would be—"

"Please. Immediately. Go and find me a railway timetable for Europe. It must have a complete set of times for western Germany. Forgive me, my friend, but there is no time for questions. Go now. Please! Now!"

Watson shook his head but hurried off and returned within a few minutes with thick, paperbound volume.

"I guess," he said, "this is Bradshaw's for Europe. Can I help you—"

"Yes. Find the pages for trains that would run from Aachen through Strasbourg and then on to Lorrach. Quickly, please."

Watson thumbed through the many pages of the directory, bending over the corners of those that applied to Holmes's demand and then handed the book over. Holmes stared at the marked pages one by one, scribbling notes and numbers as he did so. When he was finished, he shook his head.

"It cannot be done," he said.

"What cannot?" said Watson.

"It is impossible to move a half a million men and armaments all the way south to Switzerland in less than two weeks. It would take them almost a month. The railway tracks are single most of the way. There are not enough cars and engines and runs available. Not even if they commandeer every train available. They would face hopeless bottlenecks all along the route. They simply cannot do it."

"Ha. Well, that's the Germans for you, isn't it? All talk and bluster and useless when push comes to shove. The *boche* will do a jolly good job of defeating himself. Our British boys will be home by Christmas—"

"No, Watson. They are not incompetent. They are devious and brilliant. This revised plan with its detailed account of moving their armies south is a fake. It's a trick, and a brilliant one. That von Bernstorff man gave this to Mata Hari knowingly, with explicit instructions to pass it on to someone in Paris whom he knows, or at least suspects, is a British agent."

"Someone like us?"

"Perhaps. Or he has another one or two he relies on to deliver false intelligence back to London."

"Awfully clever chap … for a German that is. What are you going to do now?"

"Give me a minute to think."

Holmes lit a cigarette, stood up and began to stroll through the concourse of the train station. It was almost devoid of people now that the final train of the day had departed for the north coast and escape from France. Bundled up around the base of some of the pillars, entire families had elected to spend the night in the station, with the hope of being first in line for a passage the next morning. Mothers were hushing their babies, daughters were leaning against their fathers' shoulders, and boys were doing their best to appear brave and shouting insults about the Germans to each other.

Holmes returned and sat down.

"We are due for dinner at eight, are we not?"

"Well, yes, we are, but how can you do that knowing what you now know?"

"What I know, my dear Doctor, is that Mata Hari accepted my payment and did not deliver the promised results. She may well be of dubious and questionable virtue, but she will not welch on an agreement. She did not reach her current status by not keeping her word. Her word is her bond."

"Fine, but—"

"We are going to send her back to Amsterdam with instructions to get the correct plan."

"But won't that von Bernstorff chap be on to her if she goes back to him?"

"That is her problem. I suspect she is capable of besting him … when push comes to shove, as you say."

Chapter Eleven

Sending Her Back to Amsterdam

"A toast to your success," said Holmes as he raised a glass of champagne to Mata Hari. She responded in kind.

"Delighted to be of use to you, sir. Looking forward to future assignments."

"Forgive me for correcting you, madam. However, you were not *of use* to us. On the contrary, you were *used* by your dear friend, His Excellency, Johann Bernstorff."

She put her glass back down on the table. A glare of offense and indignation came across her famous face.

"And just what do you mean by that, Mr. Holmes?"

"What I mean is that you, my dear lady, were duped, tricked, deceived. He used you to deliver a fake plan to some agent here in Paris with the clear intent that it would be delivered to London. It is, frankly, no wonder he recruited you so readily. You were his fool."

"How do you know that? Johann is my friend. He would never do that to me. Prove what you are saying."

With a copy of the railways' directory in hand, Holmes patiently led her through his reasoning and conclusions. Her ability to understand and calculate train capacities was impressive. She scribbled notes and added up sums as she listened.

"So, madam," said Holmes when he had finished, "do you see what I mean? I admit that I was also taken in initially by the cleverness of the deception. Now then, we must use equally cool and calculated reason to decide how to respond."

Mata Hari gave no evidence of any intent to be cool and restrained. She struck the fine linen tablecloth with her fist, rattling the silverware.

"Why that miserable ******" she said, using a term that was insulting to his mother and lineage. "I'll kick him so hard in the ****** that he won't walk straight for a week."

(The portion of the von Bernstorff anatomy to which her finely tooled boot would be directed is left to the reader's imagination.)

"No madam," said Holmes, "that is far too weak a response. Allow me to suggest a better one."

"What!?"

"We shall return to Amsterdam, and you, using all of your, shall we say, irresistible charm and skill, will succeed in obtaining the true plan. If you succeed, his failure to keep it a secret will eventually become known to the Kaiser. His career shall be cut short, and he will be consigned to the seventh circle of *die Hölle* for at least a decade. Would you not agree that it would be a better fate than being temporarily indisposed in the manner you suggest?"

She fixed her eyes on Holmes for at least thirty seconds.

"Give me a cigarette," she said. Having lit one and taken several slow puffs, she stubbed it out in her saucer.

"Six o'clock tomorrow morning," she said. "Same trains. Be ready."

She stood up, and Dr. Watson also stood and spoke gently to her.

"My dear lady, your dinner? Shall we have something sent up to your room?"

"Thank you, Doctor, but I do not eat when I am angry. As the French say, revenge is a dish best enjoyed on an empty stomach … or something like that."

She turned and marched out of the dining room.

Watson sipped on his glass of champagne. "I dare say, Holmes, I do believe that you used her every bit as cleverly as Herr von Bernsdorff. You certainly knew which of her switches to flip."

"One must do what one must do for King and country, my friend. Now then, what do you say to something nutritious from the kitchen of the Ritz? Our second trip to Amsterdam is likely to be more demanding than our first one."

The two of them enjoyed a leisurely dinner and a glass or two of a fine claret. At half-past nine, they ascended the stairs to their rooms and bade each other a good night. Ten minutes later, Holmes, with his valise in hand, knocked on Watson's door.

"Terribly sorry to impose on you, my old friend. However, if you do not mind, I would appreciate your allowing me to spend the night in your room. I will sleep on the floor."

"What? Well, of course, but why in the world do you want to do that?"

"My room has become less than satisfactory, it seems."

"At the Ritz? That's impossible. These rooms are the best in all of Europe."

"Not when one opens the door to find a dead body in the middle of one's floor."

"Good Lord! What happened? Who is it?"

"I have not the foggiest. However, he has a Luger pistol in his hand, and I suspect he may have been shot whilst waiting in my room to kill me."

Watson was momentarily speechless. "Then get inside here where you're safe. I'll call down to the front desk and have them send for the police."

"Please, do not. Neither of us is now in danger. It would be best if he were to be found by the cleaning staff late tomorrow morning after we are long gone."

"Well, I suppose so. Although that will be a terrible shock to some poor maid who opens the door."

"My dear Doctor. We are in Paris. Maids in select hotels here have seen everything we, as Englishmen, can imagine and a multitude of things we cannot. They will be fine."

"But who was he? And who shot him? Surely you want to know that."

"I suspect that both the dead man and whoever did away with him are connected to the fellow on the ferry."

"That O'Hara chap?"

"Most likely. Anything further will have to wait. We have a task to fulfill that cannot be delayed. Sufficient unto the day and all that. Have a good night."

Chapter Twelve

Traveling as Baggage

6 August 1914, 5:50 am

olmes and Watson stood at the door of the Ritz Hotel, small overnight satchels in hand. Mata Hari appeared on the stroke of six o'clock. Although elegantly dressed for a day of train travel, she looked weary.

"My dear lady," said Watson, "are you quite all right. Did you not sleep well?"

"I have a telephone in my room," she said. "I was on it until the small hours of the morning."

"My goodness, you must have some unusual friends who enjoy conversations so late into the night."

"I have many excellent friends who do just that. But last night, I was chatting with a few of my special friends. Those who wear uniforms of the upper ranks in the French army. They were quite helpful."

"Indeed? What were they helping you with?"

"Advising me how to get to Amsterdam and back again tomorrow with two Englishmen in tow and not getting shot."

"Hmm … I suppose that is useful. But why do you need four large suitcases? You look as if you are about to depart on an ocean cruise."

"To be used to hide the two Englishmen I have in tow."

"Oh."

Once again, a bellboy from the hotel wheeled a luggage cart to a waiting taxi. Within twenty minutes, they arrived at the station.

"Watch the luggage," Mata Hari told Holmes and Watson. "I'll find us a cabin. But give me a few more gold coins before I do. I'll need to bribe them."

She returned fifteen minutes later, looking weary but smiling. "Some French dowager and her poodles will be furious when she learns she has lost her cabin, but we should be fine all the way to Lille. The trouble will come when crossing Belgium."

"Did your friends," asked Holmes, "indicate that we might have issues in Belgium?"

"They said that the German army is assaulting Liège and is confined to the south, but there are now armed German agents floating around Belgium and in Holland they're chock-a-block. You have to be prepared to deal with them. My passport is Dutch and we are neutral. But you two are their enemy and they will shoot you … unless you are prepared to shoot them first."

Neither of the men thought it appropriate to tell her about the body in Holmes's room.

Once in their cabin, Mata Hari leaned back in her chair and closed her eyes. Her perfectly lipsticked lips, however, were moving as if she was silently talking to herself.

"My dear lady," said Watson, "are you sure you are well?"

She opened her eyes and looked at him, smiling warmly. "Oh yes, Doctor. You are such a sweet man, but do stop killing me with kindness. I have a demanding role to play tonight and I am rehearsing my lines."

She continued in that pose most of the way to Lille, interrupted from time to time only to cadge a cigarette from Holmes. Except when called upon to give her one, Holmes read a book he had extracted from his satchel.

"Here Watson," he said. "I brought one for you as well. If we are to be spies during a time of war, it behooves us to know a bit about it. This one is short and written in simple words. You will enjoy it."

He handed his friend a copy of *The Art of War* by Sun Tzu.

"And what are you reading? It looks impressive."

"It's called *On War,* by some Junker Prussian."

"Learned anything yet?"

"Yes. He insists that war is a mere continuation of politics by other means. I'll let you know if he says anything else worth remembering."

The station in Lille was almost empty. No French man or woman wanted to travel across Belgium, and they were able to secure a private cabin without having to displace anyone. To the surprise of Holmes and Watson, Mata Hari insisted on having her several pieces of luggage kept in the cabin with them.

"Would it not be more convenient," asked Watson, "for those to be put in the baggage car? These railways are quite efficient in doing so, and there would be no delay worth fussing over."

"We shall need them when we enter Holland," she replied and then sloped back once again and closed her eyes. She continued to prepare for her role until the train stopped in Antwerp.

"This is the last stop," she said, "before we cross into Holland. Our first stop will be at the border. It is likely that German agents will board the train there, and they will be looking for anyone who is French, English or Russian. Before they do, both of you will need to climb up to the luggage racks and lie flat. I will place my suitcases in front of you so that you cannot be seen. You may have to stay there all the way to Amsterdam. I suggest you hurry into the station here and use the lavatory. You have ten minutes before we leave again."

"Are they allowed to do that?" asked Watson. "Isn't Holland a sovereign country?"

"Since the dawn of time, Germans believe they are entitled to do whatever they want in Holland. The Junkers are the worst."

"Will you be safe?"

"Doctor Watson, I assure you, I am exceptionally capable when it comes to getting rid of unwanted men. You do not have to worry."

"What if one of them attacks you?"

"Shoot him."

Watson looked over at Holmes, who shrugged and replied.

"It sounds like the best possible approach to take under the circumstances. I suggest you lie still and keep your service revolver in your hand."

Chapter Thirteen

The Kaiser's Agents

Forty minutes later, the train slowed as it neared the border. With surprising dexterity considering their age, both Holmes and Watson climbed up to the luggage racks and lay prone. Mata Hari lifted her collection of suitcases and placed them in front of the bodies, concealing them from sight.

The train was about ten minutes out of Roosendaal when the door of the cabin slid open, and a middle-aged man in a black suit stepped inside.

"*Stoppen,*" said Mata Hari. "This is a private cabin. Go find one in second or third class where you belong."

The man paused and looked at her and then continued to enter and sit down.

"I am traveling first-class, madam," he said, speaking in German.

"No one who can afford first-class would wear such cheap shoes. We would be ashamed to look so shabby," she said, responding in Dutch.

He glanced down at his shoes. "I have nothing whatsoever to be ashamed of."

"Of course not. That is the price paid by your parents for your existence."

"Is there some reason why you cannot be civil, madam? Here. Let me offer you a cigarette, and we can carry on a pleasant conversation."

He reached into his pocket, took out a package of German cigarettes and extended his hand toward her, smiling.

"No. I fear that they would cause my teeth to become as yellow and unsightly as yours."

He stopped smiling.

After lighting a cigarette himself, he tried again.

"Are you going to Amsterdam, madam?"

"No. To Frankfurt."

He looked puzzled. "Madam, this train does not go to Frankfurt. You are traveling in the wrong direction."

"What sort of *arschgeige* are you? Have you never heard of changing trains? The only thing you learned in school was how to make sauerkraut, yeah?"

"For a beautiful woman, you are not being at all friendly. I am merely a gentleman who is attempting to be pleasant to a Dutch woman. The Germans and the Dutch should be friends, should they not?"

"You sir, are a pig of a married man who should keep your compliments for your wife. What would she say if she knew you were trying to charm another woman with your pathetic remarks? Perhaps you will give me your name and address, and I will let her know what a swine she is married to."

His face went red. He stood up, called her a vulgar name and exited the cabin, sliding the door shut with a crash behind him.

Watson spoke up from his perch in the luggage rack.

"Well done, my lady. Jolly well done."

"Stay where you are," she said. "There will be others, and they will be worse. He will report to his superior agent, and I will have at least one more visit."

For the next hour, she was left in peace. The train stopped at the station in Rotterdam, and she departed for several minutes, returning with a small box of chocolates, some biscuits and a cup of coffee.

"Sorry gentlemen," she said to the rows of suitcases, "but it would have been hard to explain why I needed three cups of coffee. There are at least four German agents on this train. They were all getting coffees and talking about the war and how well it was going for them. I was tempted to tell them that attacking Belgium with their entire army was like a giant bragging about clubbing a baby to death, but I decided it was not a good idea."

A muffled grunt of agreement came from Dr. Watson's rack.

During the short stretch from Rotterdam to The Hague, they were only disturbed by the conductor checking tickets. He was a tall, austere-looking Dutch man in a neatly pressed uniform, and he politely requested to see Mata Hari's ticket.

He looked at the name on her ticket and then at her, and then again at the ticket.

"Mrs. Margaretha MacLeod?"

"I am, sir."

"Welcome home, M'greet. You may not remember me, but I cannot forget you. We met in The Hague when I was a young sailor. It is good to see you again. You have become very famous since I last saw you."

"My life has been very interesting. And you, Sven, are still as handsome as you were over a decade ago."

"Ah, you remember me. I am flattered."

"You treated me with kindness. You were generous when I was in need. I cannot forget a man like that."

"Are you coming home to Holland to escape the war?"

"Yes, of course, and to see my daughter."

"Wonderful. Enjoy the rest of your journey. I must caution you, though. There are several of the Kaiser's agents on this train. They will be suspicious of you when they see you have come from France. If they are rude to you, blow on this whistle, and I or one of my men will come immediately."

"Thank you, Sven. And will you come if I shoot him?"

He laughed and she joined him.

"Oh, very quickly, M'greet. Very quickly indeed."

He departed and she raised her head and spoke to the luggage racks.

"Did you hear that? I can shoot a rude German and get away with it."

Holmes said nothing, but Watson, ever the convivial fellow, replied.

"And then what will we do with him? Out the window?"

"He wouldn't fit. We'll have to stuff him in the toilet."

Chapter Fourteen

Another Nasty Colonel

s the train rolled to a stop at the station in The Hague, Mata Hari stood up and spoke again to the suitcases.

"The very few days of my youth that were happy, I spent here in The Hague. I need to send a telegram to Karl to arrange to meet him tonight, and so I shall go for a short walk whilst we are stopped. At this time of day, the train to Amsterdam has very few passengers. If you are careful not to be recognized, you could slip out for a short break and a cup of tea."

"Karl?" said Holmes from his place on the rack. "I thought the man you were meeting was Johann?"

"Karl Kroemer is his honorary consul. He finds me quite attractive as well. If Johann does not cooperate, I shall call on Karl later."

Holmes and Watson let themselves down from the luggage racks, stretched their limbs and made a dash for the station lavatories and café. Within ten minutes, they were back in their hiding places, and Mata Hari, having put her suitcases in front of them, was back in her seat.

She had picked up another book from a stall in the station and settled back with a new copy of *Sons and Lovers*. The bookseller had marked the pages that contained the salacious portions of the text, and she turned to these first. She was just starting on the passage in which Paul Morel first met Clara when the door to her cabin slid open.

A tall, impeccably dressed man in a dark suit entered. He was close to sixty years old but still fit and strikingly handsome.

"Forgive me, madam, but there is a screaming infant in the cabin to which I was assigned. Would you be so kind as to share your cabin with a gentleman who is old enough to be your father? I promise not to disturb you in the least."

He spoke in Dutch with a hint of a German accent. He did not wait for her to answer but smiled and bowed and sat down facing her.

Before she could utter any objection, he laughed softly.

"Oh ho, I see you are enjoying Mr. Lawrence's rather scandalous novel. He is quite the storyteller, isn't he?"

He seemed cultivated and well-mannered, and his boots said he was rich. "This is my first time reading him," she replied. "Have you read it? Oh, please, do not tell me what happens. Let me find that out for myself."

"I would never spoil a fine book, especially if it is being read by a lovely woman."

"You are very kind, sir. Would you like to read something yourself? I have a copy of the latest adventures of Tarzan that I purchased at the station. I expect it may be more to your taste than the sad life of Paul Morel and his mother."

"She leaned forward to retrieve a novel from her handbag in a well-practised move that exposed her bosom to whatever man could direct his gaze in her direction. She handed him the book and smiled.

84

"Why, thank you, my dear," he said. "You are very thoughtful."

She laughed impishly. "It is easy to be thoughtful when attending to the interests of a refined gentleman."

He accepted the book but did not open it. Instead, he sat and stared at her.

"You look familiar. Have we met somewhere before?"

"I wish we had, but sadly we have not. I would never forget a man like you."

He kept gazing at her face.

"Has anyone ever told you that you look very much like the most intriguing dancer in Europe, Mata Hari?"

"Yes," she laughed, "and there is a very good reason I have been told that."

"Ah, *wonderbar.* You are Mata Hari! How lucky can a man be? My wife and I have watched your performances in Paris, Berlin, Madrid and Vienna. She will be so thrilled to know that I met you in person. I shall send her a letter telling her as soon as I get to Amsterdam."

"Oh, do please send her my warm regards. Well then, are you going to introduce yourself, sir?"

"I am Colonel Dietrich Gephart."

"But you are not in uniform."

"Ah no. My days of commanding men in the field are over. I have retired from my post. These days, I am confined to doing a few special assignments for General von Moltke. It is not as thrilling as being on the battlefront, but it keeps me busy. Better to wear out than rust out, as they say."

"I'd say you do not look like you have rusted for even a day. But do tell. What sort of assignments? Can you tell me? Or are they secret? I am fascinated."

"Nothing glamorous. Only providing boring intelligence reports about people traveling across Europe."

"That's not boring at all. Do you want to hire me to help you catch spies?"

"No, my dear lady. I want you to tell me why you are returning from Paris to Amsterdam."

The tone of his voice had changed. He was no longer smiling at her. She forced a smile.

"I am Dutch. The war has begun. My country, The Netherlands, is neutral. I am going home to where I will be safe."

"A wise move, but you were not in danger in Paris, were you? Even when our army captures Paris in a week or two from now, you would be safe in your home at the Ritz. Your Dutch passport would protect you. So that cannot be your true reason for returning to Amsterdam."

"Perhaps I would be safe there, but I would feel better coming back home. Very few people know this, but I have a daughter in Amsterdam, my little Jeanne Louise. I want to be with her during these troubled times. She is still a child, and having her mother close to her would be helpful to her young heart."

"Yes, of course, your daughter. You love her so much that you have not returned home to see her for over a year. Forgive me, Mata Hari, for not believing you. So, please now tell me the truth. Why are you returning to Amsterdam?"

"I also have a personal reason. However, it is of a delicate nature, and I promised to keep it confidential."

"Of course. A man, no doubt. And if he is like all the other men whose company you enjoy, he is quite rich and powerful. Correct?"

She put on a face of coy embarrassment. "You know me too well, Colonel. Except you forgot to add handsome."

"Of course. His Excellency Johann von Bernstorff would be pleased to know that you speak so highly of him."

"I am sure he would be. He is quite heavenly company. But as you appear to know all about me already, why bother asking?"

"Only for the purpose of confirming the reports I have received."

"And now you have confirmed the reason I am going to Amsterdam."

"I did not ask you, madam, why you are going to Amsterdam. I asked why you are returning. You were there last night and met with His Excellency. You returned to Paris and delivered the package he gave you. But now you are going back there. Why?"

In spite of her best efforts to control her emotions, she felt her face losing its color and her stomach tightening. She forced a laugh.

"Johann, as I am privileged to call him, was such fine company and so very generous that I am returning to see him again. I am hoping he has another assignment for me. If you must know, I could use the money. Living at the Ritz is marvelous but rather expensive."

"Is it? But you were also observed in the company of a Mr. Sherlock Holmes. What were you doing meeting with him?"

"I do believe you have been spying on me. That is not what a gentleman does, sir."

"We were not interested in you at all, madam, until you were seen with Holmes. He is our enemy. He has already caused the collapse of our ring of agents in America and England. Two of our men have been killed when following him. So, I must know why you met with him and where he has gone after checking into his room in the Ritz last night? The truth, madam."

He had placed his hand into the pocket of his suit and taken out a small dagger. His fingers brushed across the edges of it as he held it in his lap.

She tensed but rolled her eyes and sighed. "Oh, very well, if you must know, Mr. Holmes is a wealthy, brilliant older gentleman, and I find him attractive. He finds me the same way. Do I need a better reason for meeting with him?"

"Yes. You do. He has no interest in women for the reasons you are alluding to. Now tell me the truth."

He had placed his right hand on the grip of the dagger and was pointing the tip in her direction.

"If you were following him, then why not ask your men? They were trained to be spies. I am only a dancer who enjoys the company of interesting men, even if they do act like they were neutered."

"The man who could have given me that information is dead. We assume that Sherlock Holmes killed him, and that is why he cannot report to me. Quit wasting my time. Tell me whatever you know about him. Or do I have to persuade you?"

He lunged across the cabin and grabbed her neck hard with his left hand, pushing her head back against the top of the seat. His right hand brought the dagger up against her cheek, and he touched the sharp edge of it against her skin.

She gasped and tried to cry out, but his grip on her throat cut off her breath.

"Either you tell me now, or your famous face will be cut and scarred for the rest of your life. Talk!"

A suitcase descended from the luggage rack on the opposite side of the cabin, striking him on the back of his head. He stood and spun around, dagger in hand, and was about to climb up on the seat below the rack when a gunshot sounded, and a bullet from an aging service revolver entered his upper leg. As he dropped to his knees, a walking stick from the other luggage rack swung down, its brass handle connecting with the back of his head. He dropped to the floor, unconscious.

Mata Hari let out a cry of relief as Holmes and Watson clambered down from their perches.

"Merciful heavens," said Watson. "What are we going to do with him? Can we—"

He was interrupted by the opening of the cabin door. Sven, the conductor, entered and stared, speechless, at the unconscious, bleeding German officer on the floor.

"Sven, darling," said Mata Hari. "Do close the door behind you. We have a bit of a problem, I fear. Can you help us?"

"Who are these men?" he demanded.

"Please let me introduce you to my dear friends, Mr. Sherlock Holmes and Dr. Watson. They are accompanying me to Amsterdam. And this chap is Colonel Gebhart, who is somewhat indisposed at the moment."

"What happened to him?"

"I shot him," said Watson. His hand was in his pocket, firmly gripping his revolver.

"And I relieved him of his consciousness," said Holmes. "Now then, sir, kindly advise us as to what to do with him."

The conductor looked at the three people who were standing and then again at the body on the floor, and a faint smile appeared on his face.

"We need to get him out of here before he bleeds all over my carpet."

"Can we move him to the toilet?" asked Watson.

"No, there are several people standing in the corridor. The gunshot brought them out of their cabins. But I would not object to having a *boche* tossed out of the window of my train."

"He won't fit," said Watson. "Even if we slide the window open as far as it will go, he is too big for the opening."

"The entire window can be removed. Stand aside. Madam, your hand please to hold the screws."

He took out a multiplex knife from his pocket and pulled open the screwdriver tool. Within five minutes, he had removed the screws that held the entire window in place and handed them to Mata Hari. Then he lifted the window away from the wall and laid it gently on the floor.

"Gentlemen, please," he said, leaning down to lift Colonel Gephart from the armpits. Holmes and Watson each grabbed a leg and, with considerable shuffling and grasping in the confined space, managed to line the Colonel's supine body up with the window opening.

"Back and forth and then on *three,*" said Sven.

Colonel Gephart was ejected through the window, landing on a grassy bank and rolling to a stop as the train continued on its way.

"Have we killed him?" asked Mata Hari.

"He'll recover," said Watson. "I aimed for the muscle in his leg, not an artery. He won't lose much blood. When he regains consciousness, he'll hobble to the nearest farmhouse."

"That should give us until tomorrow morning to get what we need in Amsterdam," said Holmes. "Madam, are you up to the task? You are understandably upset, I can see."

Se had sat down and was dabbing her eyes. "I shall be fine. He was such a handsome man. Had this been only a week earlier, he would have such good company for dinner. And his suit must have come from Saville Row and it's been ruined with the bullet through it. How sad."

"I needn't have worried about you," said Holmes. "How long, sir, until we reach Amsterdam?"

The conductor stopped replacing the window and checked his watch. "Thirty-five minutes."

Chapter Fifteen

Borrowing a Taxi

"**I** must say, Mr. Holmes, I have had nasty threats before from wives, but that was the first I have ever received from a husband. You are making my life interesting."

The three of them sat in the café in the Centraal Station, sipping on strong coffee and nibbling *stroopwafels*. Holmes was more interested in the task before them than in the one so recently in the past.

"Do you understand what we are looking for this time, madam?"

"Oh yes. You want the latest revisions to von Moltke's plan, giving the details for their march to Paris on one side and holding off the Russians on the other. Am I correct, Mr. Holmes?"

"Precisely."

"Unfortunately, I suspect I shall not be able to secure them so easily in the hotel as I did the counterfeit plan. I shall have to find a way to have Johann invite me to his private residence."

"We are counting on you to do that. I have complete confidence in your skills. Will you need assistance in opening his dispatch boxes?"

"No, I learned how to do that when spying on my husband. Captain MacLeod had locked boxes and drawers in which he tried to keep many secrets from me. Most concerned his debts and his mistresses. I became quite adept at opening them. If I fail, I will have to bring the entire box with me."

"I expect he would notice its absence immediately."

"Then you had better be prepared to make a run for it."

Having to accommodate her baggage, they hailed a taxi and took it the few blocks from the station to the Dam.

"This hotel will have German agents in it," said Holmes. "It would be best that Dr. Watson and I not register. We can wait for you around the corner in the *Kneipe*."

"You can wait in my room," said Mata Hari. "I will not be making use of it. I will be departing at eight. Knock on my door just before then, and you can wait all night in comfort until I return."

She checked into the hotel. Holmes and Watson found the pub around the corner, ate a light supper, and waited until nearly eight. Then they climbed the back staircase up to her room.

"My dear lady," beamed Watson. "Why you look *magnifique*. If only I were thirty years younger, I would be smitten."

"Oh Doctor, what is thirty years between friends? Who needs youth when you are handsome, cultivated and, after selling all those books, acceptably rich? In the spring, after this silly war is over, I shall expect an invitation to visit you in London."

She placed a light kiss on his cheek, making sure not to press too hard as it would mar her perfectly applied Guerlain lipstick, and departed.

Watson settled back into a comfortable chair and read his copy of *Trent's Last Case*. Every so often, he giggled quietly.

"Holmes, you really must read this story. I never knew that tales of detectives could be so amusing. This poor chap ends up falling in love with his suspect and making a total spike-bozzled mess of his case. I dare say, I shall have to write a story like this of one of your old cases."

Holmes was pacing the floor and smoking one cigarette after another. He stood still for a moment.

"My dear old Watson. I did not serve as a consulting detective so that readers could have a laugh at my expense."

"Oh, come now. You must admit that thinking of Sherlock Holmes being dressed as a nonconformist clergyman and being getting carried into Irene Adler's house in Briony Lodge and then dumped on her couch is good for a laugh. And then she bested you. She—"

"Enough, Watson. I have to concentrate on the task at hand."

"What task? The lady is doing all the work. All we have to do is sit and wait and hope."

"The task, my friend, is how to get out of here, across Belgium and back to England without being shot."

"Oh, well, yes, I suppose that is important. I'll let you know if this Trent fellow has any inspiring ideas."

Holmes returned to his pacing. At half-past ten, Watson stretched out on the bed whilst Holmes continued to pace and smoke. At four-thirty in the morning, a faint knock could be heard over the dull roar of Watson's snoring. Holmes rushed to the door.

Mata Hari entered and pushed a sheaf of papers into Holmes's chest. Watson woke with a start and leapt up off the bed. He stared at her. Her appearance was altered from the time she departed. Her hair was unkempt, and her lipstick was either gone or smudged. The buttons on her black satin jacket were misaligned with the buttonholes.

"My dear, are you—?" asked Watson.

"No, I am exhausted. I have not had to work so hard since the days of my miserable marriage. I do expect a generous perquisite, Mr. Holmes. Johann was still weary from the night before. I had to knock on Karl's door at midnight."

"His Majesty's government will be eager to reward you for your service."

"I hope your King George is generous. Karl gave me some money as well as a bottle of disappearing ink so I could send him spy messages. But, to be fair, you should also thank the Russians."

"The Russians? What did they do?"

"They invented vodka. German men think they can swallow a pint the way they do their beer. It has wondrous effects."

"And was that what you used to put the German consul to sleep."

"That, and if you must know, the same technique that women have used since Eve sent Adam off to his dreams. While he was sound asleep, I was able to open his dispatch box and his desk. I had to hurry and copy everything I thought was pertinent. I hope I have everything you need. Now let us get out of here."

"Brilliant," said Holmes. "Whilst you were busy and our good doctor was sleeping, I inspected the back alley of this fine hotel. As I hoped, they have two fine Renault vehicles they use for transporting guests around the town."

"You not going to steal one, are you?" said Watson.

"Steal? Of course not. Only borrow. We shall drive it as far as the border and leave a note on it telling whoever finds it to return it to the hotel. Let us go. There is no time to waste. We need to get to Whitehall as soon as possible."

With all three of them bearing a suitcase in each hand, they descended the stairs and emerged into the dark lot behind the hotel. Two large vehicles, identical to the taxis used in Paris, were sitting unattended.

Chapter Sixteen

Crossing Belgium in the Dark

"There's a chain and padlock on the hand crank," observed Watson. "Can you open it?"

"Give me a minute. Are you prepared to drive? You did so well a few nights ago?"

Holmes unchained the starting crank and, with Watson manning the throttle, they started the large Renault motorcar. It was a spacious vehicle, with room for eight people or three people and a large stack of suitcases and three jerry cans filled with petrol.

A few minutes before five o'clock on the morning of 7 August, they pulled out of the lot behind the hotel and began their run for the border. First light emerged along the eastern horizon as they worked their way out of the still-sleeping city and joined the road to Utrecht. When they reached Gorinchem at the edge of the Boven Merwede, they stopped at a café for a breakfast of coffee, eggs and *ontbijtkoek*. At seven o'clock, they put the motorcar on the ferry, crossed the river, and continued south toward the Belgian border. So far, no one had hindered their travel, and there had not been a German in sight.

The hour was approaching nine o'clock when they stopped at the village of Hazeldonk, the last stop before the border with Belgium. At the café, three older men were sitting around an outdoor table chatting, smoking and sipping coffee.

"Let me go and talk to them," said Mata Hari. "I grew up around men like this. They do little legitimate work and sit around every morning complaining about their wives, cursing the government and lying about fishing. They can help us."

She strolled over to the table and caused every one of the balding heads to turn in her direction. She sat down, and within a few minutes all of them were laughing together. After that she returned to Holmes and Watson.

"They say that there are German agents hanging around the border, and they are refusing to allow most people to cross. These fine Dutch gentlemen, however, will take us a mile up the road to where we can cross, and then they'll lead us to where we can catch the train to Lille."

"How much did you have to pay them?" asked Watson.

"I told them they could keep the car."

"Madam! You cannot do that. It is not ours to give them. That … that would be theft."

"Oh, Doctor. At ease, please. I told them they could drive around in it for a week and then would have to take it back to the hotel. They could never keep it. Everyone in the village would know it was stolen, and one of them will tell the police. And by then, we shall be long gone."

"Oh … well then, I guess that is acceptable. Are they ready to go now?"

"As you can see, they are not what one would call busy men."

Holmes checked his watch. "Have them get in the car immediately."

Following the instructions of the self-appointed leader of the trio, they drove east for a mile and then turned into what at first

96

appeared to be a grove of trees. The branches parted, and they drove slowly along a tractor path until the trees vanished and they entered a field of grain.

"Welcome to Belgium," said their guide. "We follow this path until we reach a gravel road. Turn right, and in two kilometers, we will be at the Meer station."

Their guides were reliable. In a few minutes, they approached the nearest station on the Belgium side of the border with Holland.

"Jolly good," said Watson. "Fine old chaps. How do they know this route so well?"

"Clearly," said Holmes, "they are experienced smugglers. Every border within Europe has men like this up and down the line."

At the tiny station, the questionably legal but highly useful trio of aging Dutchmen helped carry their baggage up to the platform and wished them bon voyage.

"When is the next train?" asked Holmes. "It will soon be noon. Watson, would you mind checking the posted schedule?"

"My friend," said Watson, "it does not matter what the posted times are. The next train will arrive when it arrives. Don't you know, there's a war on?"

At half-past twelve, a train going north from Belgium into Holland arrived, stopped for a minute and moved on. Holmes read the notes Mata Hari had procured during the night whilst she and Watson read their books. It was another hour before one heading south toward Antwerp and Ghent arrived. They entered an otherwise empty first-class cabin in which a previous passenger had left a newspaper. Holmes picked it up.

"The walls are closing in," he said. "That old fool, Franz Joseph, has declared war on Russia. If his troops ever get very far into Russia, they better get out before winter sets in. The Germans dropped bombs from an airship on civilians in Liege and are moving to occupy it. Ah, here's some good news. Our BEF is on its way and will start arriving in Calais today."

"Will that make it difficult for us to get through Calais and back to Dover?" asked Watson.

"I should think not," said Holmes. "They will commandeer every available ferry to bring the boys across, and we should be able to find a place on one of them. But with all the time we have lost, we have no hope of catching one before tomorrow."

"Anything interesting from our ladyship's notes?"

"Much. And it is imperative that we get this data to Whitehall straight away. It seems that the speed with which the Czar mobilized his massive army and moved it up to the Prussian border surprised the Kaiser. His generals have had to shift thousands of troops away from the west and across the country to stop their advance. That's good. That will weaken them a little as they march the mass of their men through Belgium and try to encircle the French. They were also surprised that feisty little Belgium denied them free passage and is prepared to fight."

"Anything about the French attacking Alsace?"

"Yes. Bad news. The Germans have artillery and machine guns ready to turn on the French. They'll be cut to ribbons."

"Anything else?"

"An exceptional cache of data on troop numbers, locations, planned movements, supply divisions." He looked over at Mata Hari. "Madam, you did an excellent job copying all this information in the time you had. Well done."

She lifted her head from her book. "Oh, thank you. I did go to school, you know. Of course, that was to be trained to teach kindergarten. But learning how to print neatly and quickly is finally of some use."

Progress crossing Belgium was slow. At every major stop, a young Belgian soldier boarded the train and walked the length of it, requiring passengers to show their passports. They were looking for Germans and Austrians, but anyone who did not have a current passport or acceptable papers was forced off. As those unfortunate passengers were leaving, scores of Belgians struggled to get on. The word had gone out that the Germans were attacking, and these folks and families were the leading edge of a wave that would grow and grow over the next few weeks.

When they were stopped in Antwerp, one young lad in a private's uniform recognized Mata Hari's true name on her passport and smiled at her.

"I shall tell my grandfather I met you," he said. "He is old and crippled now, but he adores you."

"Do send him my love," she said. "Judging by his fine-looking grandson, I'm sure he was a stallion in his youth."

The lad blushed and grinned. "I will tell him that for certain. It will make him very happy."

The train did not start up until every passenger had been checked. The same routine was encountered in Ghent, Waregem, Kortrijk and at the French border. It was eight o'clock in the evening before they arrived in Lille. By that time the train was packed with people fleeing Belgium and hoping to reach safe harbor in England. At the Lille station, the train disgorged its occupants onto the platform, and confusion abounded as desperate families tried to make arrangements to book transit to England.

"Gentlemen, with regret, I must bid you adieu," said Mata Hari as they stood on the crowded platform. "I shall return now to Paris, and I wish you safe travels. It has been an interesting adventure. Do call on me again if you need my richly rewardable services."

She gave them both a kiss on the cheek, smiled at Watson, shrugged at Holmes, and found her way to a taxi stand.

Holmes turned to Watson. "A very talented woman. A master of dubious means, indeed."

"She did warn you that *the woman,* Irene Adler, is her hero."

"No need to remind me. Come now, we have to get ourselves back to England."

Chapter Seventeen

Reporting to London

The two men found a small inn near the station in which to retire for a few hours. At six o'clock the next morning, Saturday, the eighth of August, they edged their way onto the first train to Calais. Even at that hour, it was packed with French people of all ages and classes trying to flee the onslaught they feared was coming from the east. Holmes and Watson stood for the entire three hours it took to travel up to the coast.

Calais was in utter pandemonium. Boats were arriving every half hour, bearing hundreds of soldiers of the British Expeditionary Force along with their horses, artillery and supplies. As the armed forces tried to move away from the piers, those wanting to board the ships pushed past them in the other direction.

"How many men," Holmes asked Watson, "do we have in the BEF?"

"I read that there are about one hundred and twenty thousand. All volunteers and all trained. Best trained army anywhere in the world, I'd say."

"Both the French and the Germans have over a million, and Russia is mobilizing three million. Why do we have so few?"

"Because we have a navy. The great oaken wall of the Royal Navy is more than enough protection for our sceptered isle. Britannia rules the waves and all that. We haven't needed a land army in decades."

"But now we do."

"These lads are the finest you can find. Any one of them is as good as five jerries."

Holmes looked at Watson in friendly condescension. "You appear to have forgotten your maths, my friend. Even if you are correct, the numbers are still highly in favor of the Germans when we run up against them."

"Oh, yes, well then, we shall just have to sign up more boys and bring all the rest we need from Canada, Australia and New Zealand. Oh, and let us not forget India. They can send us more men than the entire Triple Alliance put together."

"Good. We are going to need them."

Having obtained tickets for the early ferries, they joined the madding crowd and pushed and jostled their way to the gangplank and boarded the boat. As they pulled away from the pier, they looked out into the Channel to see an armada of Royal Navy ships approaching them. The BEF was on its way to Europe. They would take the fight to the *boche.*

They arrived back in Dover by noon and hurried to the train station.

"I say, Holmes," said Watson, "did we only leave England five days ago? Rather a busy few days, don't you agree?"

"Indeed it was. And once again, I am grateful for your assistance."

"Happy to help and happy to be back in Britannia, and happy not to have any more Germans to deal with, dead or alive."

"Well said, my old friend. As soon as I deliver all this data to the SIS, I shall be free to return, finally, to my bees and my cottage on the Sussex Downs. I do hope you will pay a visit at your earliest convenience."

"What about in a fortnight?"

"Splendid."

By noon, they had completed their crossing, and by three o'clock they were back at Victoria.

"It's Saturday afternoon," said Watson as he looked around for a taxicab. "Will those chaps at the SIS be working?"

"They better be," said Holmes. "There's a war on. I sent them a wire from Dover telling them we would be reporting."

They were let out at the same back entrance of Whitehall where they had deposited Von Bork a week earlier. The same gray man who had greeted them then opened the door in response to their knock.

"Oh, hello, Mr. Holmes. Wait here, please. I'll let Colonel Mountford know you have arrived."

He turned and vanished into the labyrinth of corridors and offices.

The same colonel they had met before arrived ten minutes later.

"Awfully sorry to have kept you waiting," he said, "but the director is frightfully busy as you can imagine."

"With good reason, no doubt," said Holmes. "He will be pleased to know that we have been busy as well."

"And your service to His Majesty is deeply appreciated regardless of how your report is received. I trust that you will not be offended to find that someone has stolen your thunder. These things happen, but we are all in it together. Every one of us has our oar to pull. This way, please. Follow me."

He led them into the office of Captain Smith-Cumming and gestured toward the chairs in front of the desk. The director was scribbling something on a paper and did not look up.

"Be with you in a minute," he said, speaking to his desk.

Chapter Eighteen

Rejected by the SIS

S̸mith-Cumming put down his pen and looked up at Holmes and Watson.

"Welcome back, Mr. Holmes. I trust you had a pleasant time in Paris with …what was her name … oh, yes, Madam Mata Hari."

"We also enjoyed our two trips to Amsterdam and back. It was a highly productive engagement."

"Jolly good. I assume you have prepared a report for us?"

"I have. Shall I tell you the most salient points?"

"Oh, not necessary. I've already heard them. All of them."

"I beg your pardon?"

"No offense, Mr. Holmes, but it's the principle of redundancy. If an army needs one hundred rifles, you make sure they have two hundred. One must be prepared for every contingency. And you, my good man, were not the only agent we had in France, and the report you are about to deliver was given to us Thursday. My men have been going over it with a fine-tooth comb since then, and we are ready to alter the plans of the BEF accordingly."

Holmes's mouth opened slightly and his eyebrows shot up.

"Pray tell, sir, what plan did you receive?"

"This one. I assume you are bringing a copy of the same document."

He held up a bound document that was lying on his desk. Holmes gasped slightly and Watson did the same, loudly.

"What, Mr. Holmes? You have seen this before, have you not?" said Smith-Cumming.

"Yes, of course I have."

"Brilliant. That's what I was hoping to hear. We're sending out word tomorrow morning to the BEF to have them start moving south to intercept the Germans forces coming across through Switzerland. Ha! They thought they could keep it secret., They'll be in for a surprise when they find us waiting for them. We'll let General Joffre know so he can reposition his men as well. Between us, we'll give those jerries a run for it."

"Sir. You cannot do that! That plan is fraudulent. It was prepared by German intelligence to fool us into sending everyone south. They are still planning to sweep through Belgium and then all the way to Paris."

"Oh, come, come, Mr. Holmes. On what basis are you saying that?"

"On what was found in the home and dispatch box of the German consul in Amsterdam."

"Found? By whom? By your favorite courtesan, perhaps?"

"Yes. Those notes are accurate and the plan in your hand is a blind."

"Is it? It does not look counterfeit to me. Here. Take a look." He handed the document across to Holmes. "I've had my chaps examining it, and they assure me that it is authentic. Same printing, same paper as other documents we purloined from the Germans. Same language. Even a few favorite phrases of Chancellor Bethmann Hollweg himself."

Holmes opened and leafed through the document. A few pages in, he stopped. The color left his face as he gazed at the lead paragraph.

"Sir, this plan is not a copy of the one I obtained a few days ago. It is the exact same document. There is a pencil tick mark right here," he said pointing his finger to a spot on the page. "I made that mark. This is a trick. They are fooling you."

Smith-Cumming stiffened in his chair.

"Mr. Holmes, I do not like being called a fool. If I have to choose between the careful analysis of an entire team of brilliant scientists from Cambridge and the greatest harlot in Europe, there is no question. Allow me to thank you for your time and service, Mr. Holmes. Enjoy your retirement in Sussex. Now, if you will excuse me, there's a war on."

"Sir! You must examine the contents of this report. It is impossible to carry it out."

"Mr. Holmes, I have thanked you for your work. A generous payment will be sent to you. Good-day, sir. Colonel, will you please see these gentlemen out. Thank you."

Colonel Mountford stepped forward. "This way, please. Be good chaps and come along. The director has another meeting to attend. Now, please."

Shaking his head in disbelief, Holmes followed the colonel out of the director's office. Watson followed them. Once they were standing in the corridor, Holmes confronted Colonel Mountford.

"Colonel, sir, do you understand the implications of what will happen if Britain and our allies adapt in response to that fraudulent plan? The war will be over by Christmas, and we will have lost."

"An excellent point, Mr. Holmes. I shall review the notes you left as well as the plan we received on Thursday and bring any concerns to the captain's attention."

"Where, Colonel, did that plan come from? It is the exact same document I reviewed a few days ago in France. Who gave it to you?"

"The director has several other agents working in Europe. Since you are all on the same team, it would not hurt for you to know who you are working alongside of. The chap who obtained the plan is a navy fellow. O'Hara was his name. You'll have to have a chat with him sometime. Brilliant chap. Ah, but you are now on your way back to Sussex, and I believe he has been sent back to France. I'll have to arrange drinks together when the war is over. Do have a good day, sir."

He escorted them out of the building and closed the door behind them.

Holmes walked a few yards along the pavement and then stopped and lit a cigarette.

"I cannot let this situation rest, Watson. This is maddening. How am I going to get through to them?"

Watson nodded slowly, and even though he knew that Holmes was using him as a listening post and was not expecting an answer, he offered one.

"What about your brother?"

"Mycroft?"

"Do you have another one?"

"No … no, of course not. But, well, yes, as they say, any port in a storm. He will be in his club now."

"Isn't he there all day every day these days? He has retired from his position, has he not?"

"He has but his position never had anything to do with his power and influence. It was all about his knowledge. He knows everything there is to know about every action, past and present, whether regrettable or heroic, of every member of the Commons or Lords. *Scientia potentia est* as Bacon noted. Mycroft has useful *scientia* in abundance. An excellent suggestion, my friend. Come. To Pall Mall."

Chapter Nineteen

Number Ten

"Good lord, Sherlock! What is it this time?" Mycroft Holmes thundered as he staggered into the Stranger's Room of the Diogenes Club. He was approaching his seventieth year and was still overweight, now requiring a cane to move slowly around the halls and rooms of the club. His eyes, however, had not dimmed as he glared at his younger brother.

"I thought," he continued, "that you had decamped to the Sussex Downs and were now wasting your life observing the sex life of bees. I'm sorry, but I know nothing about bees, nor do I ever want to."

He lowered his large frame into one of the well-padded and sturdily constructed armchairs.

"It has been over two years since I have attended to my hive," said Holmes. "I did let you know that I was in America."

"Right, so you did. Infiltrating the latter-day Fenians and I heard you were doing some espionage work. Is that why you're here?"

"It is, and I am in need of your help. To be precise, England is in need of your ability to persuade our highest government officials to change their war plans and do so immediately."

"Appealing to my jingoistic patriotism, are you? Very well, it's better than trying to bribe me. Proceed."

Holmes gave an account, precisely and quickly, of his escapades over the past few days, noting how he had succeeded first in obtaining a false plan and then acquiring accurate data.

"Do you do that all by yourself?" asked Mycroft.

"I have some help here and there."

"From whom?"

"A very capable Dutch woman. Her name is Margarethe Zelle MacLeod."

"What!? You employed Mata Hari!?"

"I believe that is the stage name she now uses."

Mycroft leaned back in his chair and roared with laughter.

"Well, I must say, dear little brother, that shows a splendid use of your imagination. Well done. There is hope for you yet."

"By your reaction, I take it you know her, or at least about her."

"Of course, I know her. So do at least a dozen members of the House of Lords and a quarter of the members of White's and Boodles. A much better choice of agents than some pointy-headed scholar from Cambridge. It is a truth universally acknowledged that a man cannot think at one and the same time with his big head and—"

"Yes, brother. I am aware of that truth. And now, please listen whilst I explain why the plan the director is now relying on must be a blind."

Holmes recited verbatim the paragraphs from the *Aufmarsch III Westen* document that called for the movement of the bulk of

German troops from the border of Belgium down to the south and the secret plan to have them cross through Switzerland and attack France from the south.

Mycroft listened, sipping on a generous tumbler of single malt scotch. As soon as Holmes had repeated the plans for troop movements, he slammed his glass down on the side table.

"Stuff and nonsense. The rail capacity through western Germany could not possibly accommodate that many troops. Those lines through Alsace and Lorraine are all *Sekundärbahn* and *Vizinalbahn*. They would be better to march their armies south. But even if they force-marched them fifty miles a day, it would take them ten days to get them there. Utterly impossible!"

"Thank you, dear brother. But that is the plan now believed by the SIS. They are about to instruct the Field Marshall French and the BEF to turn south and to share their so-called intelligence with the French and get them to do the same thing."

"Complete idiocy," said Mycroft. "They'll leave no resistance at all in the north. The Germans will have a cakewalk through Belgium, Flanders and Picardy. They'll be in Paris in a week."

"Precisely. Now do you see why I need your help?"

Mycroft closed his eyes, sipped on his scotch, and slowly shook his head from side to side.

He let out a long, slow sigh. "Well then, if I must, I must."

He leaned forward and placed his flabby hands on the arms of his chair. With considerable strain, he lifted his body until he was standing.

"There should be a cab out on Pall Mall," he said.

"So there should," said Holmes. "Where are we going?"

"Number Ten."

Chapter Twenty

A Friend of the Prime Minister

Holding onto the railing of the steps of the Diogenes Club, Mycroft Holmes slowly descended to the pavement. He took one step at a time, making sure that both feet were securely on the tread of one step before lowering his foot to the next one.

Watson held his forearm as he dropped his wide backside into the cab. Once they reached number ten Downing Street, Watson hurried to the door of the cab and extended his hand to help pull Mycroft Holmes to his feet.

There were several police officers patrolling the street and one stationed beside the door. Mycroft ignored all of them and gave the door a sharp series of knocks with his cane. It was opened by a tall, gaunt gentleman in the starched dress of a butler.

"I am sorry, sir," he said to Mycroft, "but no one is permitted in this residence without an invitation from the Prime Minister. If you leave your name and address, one of his secretaries will be in contact with you."

"You will go and tell Little Herbie that Mycroft Holmes needs to meet with him immediately."

The butler was noticeably surprised.

"Are you, indeed, the Mycroft Holmes?"

"There is no other. Now go and fetch Herbie and bring him here."

"Very good, sir. Please step inside."

The man turned and climbed the long staircase to the second floor and disappeared. Mycroft addressed Holmes and Watson.

"Asquith was a few years behind me at Balliol. He read classics but was quite a good debater. That was the name we pegged him with when he arrived still wet behind the ears."

"A good thing," said Holmes, "that the opposition members in the Commons are not aware of it. Otherwise he might never live it down."

"If he cannot do a better job of rallying the country to fight the war, he will not be around long anyway."

"But rather a bright chap, from what I've heard," said Holmes.

"Best described as perceptive, perspicacious and priapic."

A handsome man, formally dressed and of the same age as Holmes and Watson, appeared at the top of the staircase.

"Mycroft Holmes," he said loudly. "What in the name of all that is holy has roused you out of your soft beds of luxury and brings you out. It must be something dreadfully serious, or you would never venture beyond Carlton."

"It is of supreme importance, otherwise I would not be here, and you know that, Herbie."

"Very well, then. Come up and we'll talk."

Mycroft Holmes ran his gaze up and down the long staircase.

"No, it would be better if you would come down. We can chat in your parlor."

The Prime Minister of England shrugged and started down the stairs. Another man, considerably younger, followed him, as did an attractive young woman who could not have been more than twenty-five years old. On reaching the bottom of the stairs, he gestured to the chap behind him.

"Have you met my First Lord of the Admiralty? We were in the middle of a session about how best to deploy the Fleet. He's quite bright, and he may as well join us."

He did not introduce the young woman.

"Aren't you," asked Mycroft, "the self-described, self-congratulatory hero who escaped from the Boers?"

"That I am. The name is Churchill. However, my friends call me Winnie."

"Good to know, Mr. Churchill. What I have to say will be of interest to the Royal Navy, so come in and listen carefully. I assume you have heard about my brother."

He pointed to Sherlock Holmes.

"As a boy at Harrow, I read all those stories about him."

"Good, well sit down and listen to what he has to tell you. And when he's finished, you will need to send instructions to the fleet as well as the BEF."

The butler appeared, bearing a tray of glasses and two decanters, one with port and the other with scotch. He poured a drink for each of the five men and left the decanters on the side table beside Churchill.

The brothers Holmes succinctly explained the issues that had arisen and the contents of both the false plan and the notes obtained in the residence of the German Consul in Amsterdam.

"How did you get hold of all these documents, Mr. Holmes?"

"I was assisted by an exceptionally capable agent."

"Indeed? What's his name?"

"*Her* name, sir, is Margarethe Zelle MacLeod."

"Mata Hari? She helped you? Bless her. Isn't she something? Oh my, we shall have to chat about her later. For now, tell me where these notes and this plan are now."

"In the office of Captain Smith-Cumming," said Holmes. "To the best of our knowledge."

"Wait here," said the Prime Minister. He stood and left the room, returning a minute later.

"I've sent one of my men over to Whitehall to retrieve those notes. As soon as they get here, I shall review them. Until then, we have other business to attend to."

He and the First Lord of the Admiralty left the parlor. The young woman remained behind and graciously smiled at the three men.

"It is an honor to meet you," she said.

"As I suppose it is for us to meet you, Miss Stanley," said Mycroft.

"Oh my goodness, you know who I am?"

"I do not know you as well or in the same way as H H does, but you are known to be one of his trusted advisors. Between you and Churchill, I am hoping you can stiffen his spine regarding a robust response to the Germans."

"I promise to do my best to stiffen his response, as you say, sir," she said and winked at Mycroft. "Please, relax. I recommend that you make yourself at home. H H enjoys making his guests comfortable."

She smiled again at the men and departed.

"And who might she be?" asked Watson.

"Her name is Venetia Stanley," said Mycroft. "Herbie writes letters to her when his cabinet meetings bore him, which is most of the time. She is his *great friend.* Beyond that, don't ask."

"Wouldn't think of it," said Watson. "So, what happens now? Do we just sit here?"

"In a word," said Mycroft, "yes."

They waited. After no more than a minute, Mycroft told Watson to pull on the bell chord, whereupon one of the household staff appeared.

"I am feeling somewhat peckish," said Mycroft. "I'm sure this place has the ability to make up some sandwiches and can find a decent port. Kindly see what you can organize."

In seven minutes, a plate laden with sandwiches and a decanter of port appeared. Holmes and Watson ate lightly, Mycroft not so much. Then they waited again.

After another fifteen minutes, they heard the door of Number Ten open and close and the rapid steps of an obviously fit, young man as he leapt up the stairs, taking two or three in each stride. Then there was silence again.

Twenty minutes later, Herbert Asquith and Winston Churchill descended the stairs and entered the room. Watson and Holmes stood to greet them. Mycroft remained in his chair.

"Gentlemen," said the Prime Minister, "we have reviewed the documents in question. Mr. Churchill agrees with you that the plan printed to appear like a publication of the Kaiser is undoubtedly a false one, constructed to fool us. Thank you for bringing it to our attention. The notes on the most recent pieces of intelligence and changes in plans of the German army all across Europe are most useful. On behalf of His Majesty, thank you. You have made an invaluable contribution to the war effort. Do enjoy the rest of the weekend. Best wishes, Mr. Holmes on your return to Sussex."

"May I be permitted a question?" asked Holmes.

"One," said Asquith.

"Does the data we have provided you give our side the advantage allowing us to press our attack? It is my hope that it would."

"No, Mr. Holmes, it gives us the advantage of retreat."

"Sir?"

"It is too early to say what tactics will win this war, but look at what happened yesterday to the French when they tried to advance into Alsace. They met withering fire from rifles and machine guns and lost twenty-seven thousand men in one day. It appears that the advantage is to the army defending rather than attacking. Your notes will most likely convince Generals French and Joffre that a strategic retreat in which the advancing army suffers far more losses than the retreating one may be a useful strategy. Time will tell."

They exchanged parting pleasantries, and the Holmeses and Dr. Watson departed. Mycroft, with some difficulty, lowered himself into a cab.

"Sherlock, I am returning to my club. Let me know if you need me again, but please, not too soon."

He departed in the direction of Pall Mall.

"Holmes, old friend," said Watson, "you are welcome to spend the night in our home on Queen Anne Street. It is not far from here."

"Good old Watson, thank you. I believe that my final mission has been completed. I shall return to my bees tomorrow morning. I have sorely missed them."

Chapter Twenty-One

Recruited by the French

At the station in Lille, Mata Hari boarded a train back to Paris. She was one of only a handful of passengers returning to the City of Light. No one recognized her or even spoke to her. At the Gare du Nord, she found a taxicab, and by nightfall she had returned to the Ritz Hotel in the Place Vendôme.

The square in front of the hotel was quiet. As she stood there alone, she turned around and gazed at the splendid column that honored the triumphs of Napoleon at Austerlitz. It had been knocked down during the Commune but was restored and had stood in its place for the past forty years, a monument to the glories of *La France.* She quietly said a prayer that it would not be toppled again in the darkening days that were descending on her beloved city.

Now somewhat flush with funds, she strode straight away to the office of the hotel manager.

"Bonsoir ma chère dame, he said as she entered. "You have been absent these past two nights. I hope there has not been any problem here for you. To what do I owe the honor of your visit."

"I have come to update my account," she said. "I believe I owe you a few francs. I know it is a paltry sum, but it is my desire to be on the best of terms with my favorite establishment."

"*Mais oui, madam*. It is so good of you to come and offer. In the past, we have not pressed you to make a payment as your presence here was such a magnificent advertisement for us. No end of men and women of means chose to stay here because they heard it was blessed by your recommendation. Sad to say, those days are over. Those men and women fled the minute war was declared. Now our accounts are under duress. You are so very thoughtful to think of us."

The sum owed was not paltry at all. It depleted all the money paid to her by Sherlock Holmes and a portion of the advance given by the German consul. Invitations for her exotic dance performances had vanished. Generous men of substantial means and easy virtue were fleeing the city. An alternative source of funds had to be found.

"*Un moment, madam,* before you go. We have received a notice from our friends at 282 Boulevard Saint-Germain. They have told us that all of our guests who are foreign nationals must go there and register. Forgive me, madam, I know it is an inconvenience, but I must ask you to comply."

"It is not a problem. I will go."

After a delectable *petit déjeuner* at the Ritz the following morning, she walked through the empty Jardin des Tuileries and across the Pont de la Concorde to the far side of the Seine. Although it was summer and the weather warm, she dressed in a dark-colored suit and sported a straw hat with a large brim, above which floated a grey plume.

The door of the Military Bureau for Foreigners was open and she entered. The interior was austere, and most ordinary citizens found the place intimidating. Mata Hari, however, floated through with the easy gait of an artist, habituated to walk into a scene and commanding attention. Once inside, she was directed to an office on the second floor.

"*Bonjour madam*," said the beaming official. "We have been expecting you."

"And of course, I have come as has been required of all Dutch people living in Paris. Is there something I have to sign? Are you going to take a photograph of me? I have brought some very good ones to save you the trouble? Am I required to pay a fee to be able to stay in Paris?"

"Oh, no, madam. Nothing like that. However, I have received a note saying that when you appeared, I was instructed to send you to a private meeting in the *Deuxième Bureau*. Monsieur Georges Ladoux has requested to meet with you. There is no need for concern, madam. He is a charming man."

She waited briefly outside the office of this M. Ladoux until she was asked to enter. As she did, she remembered to swing her hips ever so slightly, like the trained dancer she was. She needed a favor from this man, and she knew how to obtain it.

"Welcome, madam," said Ladoux. "How may our humble office be of assistance to the famous Mata Hari?

"I only came here to register, but they have sent me to you. As they chose to do so, then I shall ask a favor of you?"

"And what is that, madam?"

"It is August. No one with any elan remains in Paris in August. I wish to travel and take the waters for a few weeks."

"Do you now? And where do you wish to go?"

"To Vittel."

Oh, madam, I cannot allow you to go there. It is too close to the war front. All of our officers would be in danger of being seduced by you and rendered ill-equipped to fight. That would never do."

"That would not be a problem. I have fallen in love with a Russian gentleman here and am entirely faithful to him."

"Ah yes, Vladmir Godina-Kuznetsova. We have seen you dining with him at the Tour d'Argent. And have you, by chance, also fallen in love with Mr. Sherlock Holmes?"

She laughed. "Him? No. No woman will ever love him because he refuses to love a woman. He is only in love with his bees."

"Yes, so we have heard. But all the same, a journey to Vittel is not possible. But please do not be disappointed. I have an alternative to propose to you."

"Yes?"

"What would you say to a travel permit to Geneva? Swiss men can be very handsome, can they not?"

"They are the most arrogant on earth. They think they can win a woman with a box of chocolates. Why would I want to meet a Swiss man when French men are so much more interesting and cultivated?"

"Why? Because there may be a reward in store for you by going to Switzerland."

He paused and let his words be considered. She considered his words.

"Go on."

"As a Dutch national, you could then travel from Geneva to Berlin. You have many friends in Berlin, do you not?"

"Go on."

He laid in front of her an offer unlike any she had received in her life, with the exception of the one made to her a few days earlier by the German consul in Amsterdam. Ladoux wanted her to spy on the Germans for the French.

"How much will you pay me?"

"How much do you want?"

"One million francs."

"Oh, *mon dieu*. That is far beyond my account, but if you continue work on our behalf until the war is over, *La Republique* will be very generous.

They negotiated a fee that would provide her with freedom from financial worries for years to come. She neglected to mention that she was also being employed by the Germans for similar services.

"When do I leave?"

"We will need a week or two to make all the necessary arrangements in Geneva to welcome you there. We want you to be seen to be living well."

"Is there any other way?"

Chapter Twenty-Two

Bees Notwithstanding

Around noon on the twenty-fifth of August, a small Ford puttered through Pevensey and continued on a secondary road until it reached the gate of a small farm. The name on the gate read *S. Holmes, Apiarist.* Dr. John Watson turned into the laneway and rolled up to the farmhouse.

The view was unparalleled. From the porch of the house, one could look out over the great chalk hills and across the Channel to the coast of France. The several acres that surrounded the house supported small groves of fruit trees, flowering shrubs, cultivated flower beds and rolling hills festooned with wild flowers. Scattered amidst the vegetation were nearly one hundred beehives, organized into lots of six or seven.

"Ah, good old Watson," a voice called from inside the house. Sherlock Holmes emerged, casually dressed, a pencil stuck behind his ear, and his fingers smudged with ink.

"Capital of you to come, old sport. Do come in and join me for a glass of claret. Or shall I welcome you with a tour of my hives? Those buzzing little fellows would positively swarm to greet you."

"A glass of wine would be fine," said Watson.

The two of them sat by the unlit hearth, talked about the weather and asked about each other's health. Then Watson gave in to his curiosity.

"You must tell me, Holmes. What has come of your second book?"

Holmes could not repress a grin and got up and walked into his pantry. He returned bearing a cardboard box and placed it on the coffee table. It bore the name of *Constable & Co., Publishers* and was packed full of new books. Out of it he extracted a single copy and handed it to his friend.

"Archibald Constable has just yesterday delivered this to me. I confess I am rather proud of it."

The book bore the title, *Practical Handbook of Honey Production, with Some Observations upon the Efficacy of Honey for the Preservation of Masculine Proclivities.*

"Capital, just capital!" enthused Watson. "Archie Constable must love it. He has not had a decent book to flog since Bram Stoker wrote his silly nonsense about Transylvania."

"I should hope so," said Holmes. "Shall I read you a chapter?"

"No, no. No need to put yourself out. But if you will sign a copy, I shall treasure it."

Holmes picked up a pen and was about to sign the title page under his name when he was interrupted by the sound of a motorcar approaching the house. The two of them rose and stepped outside. A large Ford had pulled up to the door, and two men got out of it.

Holmes stared at them, not quite believing what he was seeing. Watson stepped down from the porch to greet them.

"I say, Colonel Mountford and Captain Smith-Cumming. What a surprise?"

"Ah, we were hoping to find you here, Dr. Watson. Hello, Mr. Holmes. Mind if we come in for a wee chat?"

Holmes said nothing but gestured with his hand to the open door.

"Do have a seat," he said once the four of them were inside. "I should like to think that the fame of my select blend of honey has reached the corridors of Whitehall, but I rather suspect I am overly optimistic and the reason for your visit is something far less delectable."

"It is," said Smith-Cumming. "Our time is hard-pressed, so I shall come immediately to the point."

"By all means," said Holmes. "No sense beating around the bush. It would tempt me to believe you worked for the government."

"Right," said Smith-Cumming. "Touché. I will get the first item out of the way forthwith. His Majesty's Secret Intelligence Service wishes to thank you for your excellent work in France and in Paris. Well done, sir. As a result of your efforts, the BEF has been able to stop the advancing Germans in Mons at least for a few days, and we are now making a strategic withdrawal."

"With the help," said Holmes, "of the terrifying descent of a band of angels dressed as St. George and a band of English yeoman soldiers armed with longbows. They held off the jerries whilst our lads pulled back in safety, more or less."

"Please, Mr. Holmes, that was a nonsense piece of fiction that has been bruited abroad throughout England and foolishly believed as if it truly took place."

"Nothing foolish about convincing the populace that God is on our side. Regardless, what do you want?"

"This woman you worked with, Mata Hari. Have you heard from her?"

"Not a word? Why?"

"We are in need of her help again."

"So are a hundred men of your age. Do be more specific."

"Bethmann Hollweg and von Moltke are constantly changing their minds. We need to know their latest plans as they march south toward Paris. Our boys are retreating, and the French are utterly on the run. We have to know if the *boche* can be stopped or if, to save lives, it would be better to pull the BEF back across the Channel and let Paris fall."

"Ah, yes. Paris may be worth a Mass, but not a hundred thousand lives. A sticky wicket, I'd say. What has Mata Hari got to do with this?"

"She is Dutch and can still travel through Geneva to Berlin. We are aware that she knows half of the German generals and cabinet, shall we say, intimately. We need to have her get to Berlin, chat up her *Jungs* and find out what they are going to do?"

"A brilliant idea. But why are you telling me all this? Why don't you go and ask her?"

"Because nobody can find her. Even you could not find her, Mr. Holmes, not withstanding all your reputed skills and intellect. Could you?"

"Of course, I could. All it takes is careful investigation, an application of disciplined reason and a modicum of imagination."

"Oh, which you still have."

"I did not lose my skills just because I have chosen to apply them to my bees."

"By jingo, I'm sure you didn't!" said Smith-Cumming. He stood and clapped his hands as he spoke. "Very well then, kindly pack your valise. You are going back to France to find her and put her to work one more time. Dr. Watson, you will be going along to tend to the removal of any bullets that find their way into Holmes."

Holmes was momentarily speechless.

"Oh no. Not having any of that here. I did my bit. Twice someone tried to kill me, and frankly six hours in a luggage rack did not do my rheumatism any good at all. So, do not even think about sending me back."

"Mr. Holmes, you are on record as agreeing to help 'for as long as I am needed.' Your words, sir. And once again we need you. His Majesty assumes that you are a man of your word. Well, are you or are you not?"

If the glare from Holmes's eyes could have been focused into a single ray of light, it would have burned a hole straight into the chest of the Director of the SIS and out the other side of his torso. He stood up, gave him one last hard look and walked out of the room onto his porch.

"Is he ...?" Smith-Cumming asked Watson.

"He is. Just like that last time. He may need three pipes. A glass of wine whilst you wait? Perhaps some honey on toast?"

Chapter Twenty-Three

Poor Little Belgium

I t took Holmes only one pipe, and he returned to his small parlor.

"There will be one condition," he said. "No, make that two."

"I cannot imagine anything to which we would object," said the director.

"One. You must find and appoint a capable apiarist to tend to my bees whilst I am away. It has taken me two weeks now to clean and restore my hives. I will not so heartlessly desert my queen again."

"Jolly good, but I have no idea where to find such a person."

"There is a directory of the Sussex Beekeepers in my office. Two. In the event that Mrs. Margaretha Zelle MacLeod is suspected of treason by any party, she must be given asylum in England."

"The House of Lords will may never recover, but I am sure that can be arranged. So, agreed."

"Brilliant. When do we leave?"

"All of the kit you and Dr. Watson will need is in the boot of the motorcar. It is a lovely two-hour drive along to coast to Dover. Shall we go?"

"One more question. Did you find and get rid of the traitor in the SIS who informed some German agent about our last mission, which nearly got us shot?"

"No. Sorry about that. You will have to keep watching your back. We are working on it."

"That is so very reassuring."

Holmes and Watson caught an evening ferry and found themselves once again standing alone on the deck as the great white cliffs faded behind them and the lights of the French coast glowed ever brighter.

"Awfully thoughtful of you to be concerned about the safety of Mata Hari, Holmes," said Watson. "Do you fear for her?"

"She is singularly capable of looking out for her own interests. In times of peace, there is naught to be lost in doing so except the occasional male friend, and they are easily replaced. In times of war, she may be her own greatest enemy. I would not be surprised if we have to save her from herself whilst trying to save both France and England from the Germans."

"How do you expect to find her when the SIS has not been able to?"

"As a private consulting detective, I have access to tools and techniques which they do not."

"Such as?"

"Bribery. Theft. Coercion. Duplicity. Deception. Shall I continue?"

"Not necessary, my old friend. I am sure that old age and treachery will defeat youth and idealism yet again."

They stood in silence for some time, looking out over the ocean and enjoying the balmy summer evening breeze.

"I was wondering," said Watson after a long pause. "About that woman. Do I detect the presence of concern that is beyond what you would usually feel for any other woman who might happen to be of assistance to you?"

"I am concerned only for her safety. I have no other feelings whatsoever."

"Hmm … that's what I thought."

The ferry pulled into the pier at Calais. As far as the eye could see, people were standing, sitting, shuffling about. There were thousands of them. Men, women, and children were thronged about the docks, all hoping to secure passage to England. The early days of the war had unleashed a multitude of refugees.

With their suitcases in hand, they wove their way through the masses, stepping over small piles of precious belongings and sleeping children as they trudged several blocks to a café near the Calais-Ville train station.

Every table in the café was occupied, and they were about to give up on a nourishing snack when a man in the corner waved at them and gestured to the two empty chairs at his table. As they approached, he stood to greet them. He was hardly more than five feet four inches tall but affected an air of dignity. His perfectly waxed mustache was stiff and military. The neatness of his attire was exceptional given the chaos of humanity he was a part of. Even the spats he wore over his patent leather boots were perfectly clean and lacking a single crease.

"Ah, thank you, sir," said Watson. "So kind of you to take pity on a couple of traveling Englishmen."

"*Mais non, monsieur,*" said the small man. "Had your being English was the only fact I observed about you, I would have ignored you. As a refugee fleeing for my life, I have enough to upset

129

mon estomac without adding a conversation with Englishmen. *Non, non, mes frères.* To you I waved because I recognize you, and my brain is wondering *pourquoi* Sherlock Holmes and Dr. Watson are here in France."

Holmes and Watson were visibly surprised. "Pray tell," said Holmes, "how is it you know who we are."

"But of course, I know who you are as I am also a detective. The cells of my brain have stored the images of everyone I had met or whose picture I have seen. Yours, I have seen many times. Therefore, it does not require much effort of my intellect, *mon intelligence supérieure,* to have reached the conclusion that you are here to assist France and England in the fight against the *boche.* Allow me to offer you a coffee and a sandwich, which are the disappointing best this café has to offer, and I shall pass along whatever knowledge I have gleaned."

"Why thank you, sir," said Watson. "We greatly appreciate the warm hospitality offered to us by our French allies."

Their host's head jerked back in righteous indignation. "*Monsieur!* Please. I am not a Frenchman. I am a citizen of Belgium."

Oh, well. My humble apologies," said Watson. "I had not expected to find so many Belgians fleeing to England."

"Ah, *mon pauvre pays.* We fought against the Germans like valiant heroes, but we were Davids against a Goliath. In such an encounter, except for the unlikely account in the Holy Scriptures, Goliath always wins. The Germans are taking revenge upon us for having the gall to fight them, and they are killing our civilians—men, women, children, babes in arms, and even the village priest—so those of us who can are fleeing, hoping to find safety on the other side of *La Manche.*"

Sandwiches and coffee arrived at their table. The detective from Belgium ate his sandwich with his knife and fork.

"I have read these reports of the German atrocities," said Holmes. "Are they true?"

"Ah, *monsieur,* but what is truth? In a time of war, it is the first to die. There is a bit of truth in what has been reported, but there is great *utilité,* and they serve in the cause of a greater truth, *n'est-ce pas?*

"Explain, please, sir."

"These stories about atrocities and angels descending and *la pauvre petite Belgique,* they are bringing together all the people of England to support the war. And your English press, they are sending these stories across the ocean to America. If there are enough stories like this and people believe them, the peaceful American president will send their boys to help us over there. *Donc,* for us these stories are true, even if they did not truly happen."

"An interesting observation, sir. But tell me, as you appear to be well-informed on these matters, how now can I get across Belgium and into Holland if I have to?"

"You cannot. The Germans have occupied almost the entire country. If you want to visit Holland, you will have to go by boat."

"Very well. Can we still get to Paris on the train?"

"*Oui,* but not for long. And if you get there, you may not be able to get back. The German army is advancing across the north of France. *Très bientôt* they will cut off the line leading to Calais. It is a risk that is very big, *non?* But if you are going to help defeat the Germans, it is worth it, *oui?*"

Chapter Twenty-Four

He Lives at the Hotel du Louvre

All trains running from Calais toward Flanders had been canceled. At seven o'clock in the evening, a train from Paris arrived at the station, and what seemed like several thousand people got off and moved *en masse* toward the docks. There could not have been more than a dozen passengers on the train back to Paris. As it rolled back through the countryside of Artois and Picardie, they took note that the fields were now devoid of farmers, and the towns appeared to have been abandoned.

The unrelenting German army had been held back at Mons and the other points along the frontier, but they could not be stopped. It was only a matter of time before they were at the gates of Paris.

The Gare du Nord was crowded but silent. Every square inch of the station was occupied by individuals and families who had bivouacked for the night, praying for a chance to board a train, any train, that would take them away from the oncoming juggernaut.

They picked their way through the squatters and found the line of taxis at the west side of the station.

"Any chance," asked Watson, "we might find that Mathieu chap again? He seemed quite reliable."

"We can look," said Holmes.

They found him. He was several back in the line, and Watson gave a franc to each of the drivers in front of him so as not to offend. Mathieu recognized them straight away and beamed a welcome.

"*Bonjour, mes amis anglais*. You have returned to Paris. You are truly mad. Where shall I take you? Back to the Ritz?"

Watson smiled back. "Yes, that would be—"

"No," said Holmes. "This time to the Hotel du Louvre."

"*Bien sûr*. It is also a very fine hotel, and all our finest *magasins* are close by. *Mais malheureusement,* some of the best ones have closed, and the owners have fled. So have almost all of the hotel guests. You will be welcome."

"Why there?" asked Watson once they were in the taxi. "I rather liked the Ritz."

"It is the only other address we have associated with Mata Hari, and as we know she is no longer at the Ritz, we may as well start our search there."

The elegant hotel was only a block from the entrance to the great museum, and its elegant lobby, supported by classic Corinthian pillars and festooned with palm trees, spoke of the grandeur of the French Empire. Except for one young man at the front desk, the lobby was empty.

"Do you think she might be here?" said Watson.

"Unlikely, but I shall ask to look at the register."

"He can't show that to you. It's confidential, isn't it?"

"Come now, Watson. He is young and French and therefore can be bribed. Do you have a few francs in your pocket? Five should be more than enough."

As Holmes had predicted, after welcoming them to the hotel, the clerk accepted the pile of coins Watson pushed in his direction and turned the register around so that Holmes could read it. He ran his finger down the column of names on the page that was open and then turned the page back to the one before it and did the same. He continued this process until he had observed the previous six months of guests who had checked in. He was about to close the register and hand it back when his gaze settled on one name. He had not seen the name of that man since 1895, when his diligent efforts resulted in the man's incarceration.

Hugo Oberstein was living in room 204 of the Hotel du Louvre.

Chapter Twenty-Five

Mr. Hugo Oberstein

"What's he doing here?" asked Watson. "I thought you had him convicted and sent off to prison."

"He was sentenced to fifteen years," said Holmes. "That was nineteen years ago. He has been free for the past four years."

The two men sat in one of the few cafés on Rue St. Honoré that was open at that hour of night sipping a *café au lait* and enjoying a *pain au chocolat* which even the threat of occupation by an enemy army could not stop the dedicated bakers of Paris from delivering fresh every morning and afternoon.

"And you think he is up to his old tricks?" said Watson.

"*Can a leopard change its spots? Neither can those do good who are accustomed to doing evil.* Jeremiah, I believe. Oberstein was a ruthless foreign agent and a murderer. I would not be surprised to learn that he still is both."

"What are you going to do?"

"Place a bait in front of him. If he ignores it, I shall ignore him. If he bites, then we have our man and a possible connection to Mata Hari. However, we have to move quickly. The German army will not wait for us to devise an elaborate plan."

Holmes sat in silence for several minutes and then called for the waitress to come to their table.

"*Mademoiselle,*" he said, doing violence to French pronunciation from the outset. He continued to do so and requested that she bring a pen, ink and a piece of paper. She did so. Then he asked if she could write neatly. She gave him an odd look but nodded.

"*Magnifique.* Watson, please put three francs on the table. This lovely young lady is going to be our secretary."

She gave a Gallic shrug and, there being no other customers to attend to, sat down and took up the pen.

Holmes dictated, and his newly-acquired secretary first translated his words and then wrote them down. In translation, the note read:

Dear Mr. Oberstein:

With regard to our recent transaction, you will no doubt have become aware that the situation in Europe is changing rapidly. It is imperative that I deliver to you the most recent version of the document I left for you two weeks ago. It is also imperative that you deliver it to your contact immediately. If you wish to continue to be paid for your services, you will meet me in the bar of your hotel at midnight tonight.

It was signed, M.H.

"That should do it," said Holmes. He thanked the waitress, and the two of them hurried back to the Hotel du Louvre. Holmes approached the front desk and requested an envelope from the cooperative clerk. Having placed the note in the envelope, he handed it back.

"Kindly deliver this at once to Mr. Oberstein. I believe he is in room 204."

"*Monsieur*, I would do that if I could, but I cannot leave the desk. I am the only person here now. The boys and maids, those who are still working here, have all gone home for the night."

"I assure you, young man," said Holmes, "that my friend and I shall protect your desk from any intruders."

"*Eh bien,* but still, it is very late. Mr. Oberstein will have gone to bed already. We are not supposed to disturb our guests unless it is an emergency."

"Ah, but it is an emergency, and you may tell him so. Watson, would you mind giving this chap a generous compensation for the trouble we are putting him to?"

Watson slid another five francs across the counter and the clerk smiled.

"I shall deliver this note and let Mr. Oberstein know that it is an emergency."

Holmes and Watson stood at the front desk, protecting it as they had promised until the lad returned.

"I had to wake him up," he said, "and he was not happy, but he said he will be right down."

"Excellent work. Thank you," said Holmes.

At ten minutes before midnight, the hotel bar was deserted, and they took a seat at a table in a dark corner.

"Holmes," whispered Watson, "she told us that she was to leave the plan document for a Mr. Smith."

"She did indeed, and up to the moment I read the name of Hugo Oberstein in the register, I believed her."

"You mean she lied to you?"

"Precisely."

"But … but she seemed to me to be telling the truth."

"Precisely, to me as well, which proves that she is an exceptionally accomplished liar. I should have realized that any woman who could convince tens of thousands of Europeans that she is a Hindu princess when she was no more than a Dutch woman from some boring village in Holland, should not be unquestionably believed. Furthermore, any woman who can manage four lovers at the same time, every one of them intelligent men of means, must be utterly brilliant at prevaricating."

"But why would she lie about Oberstein?"

"Because he represented another potential source of income, and why take a chance on losing that."

"Fine, but how can you possibly now want to work with her when she cannot be trusted?"

"The greatest skill a spy can possess is the ability to lie and do so convincingly. That, she has proven. The second requirement of a spy is that he, or in our case she, will deliver the product or service for which she is being paid and do so with superb punctuality. Frankly, I do not care a fig for whatever confection she spouts as long as she secures the data England and our allies need."

"So, all's fair in love and war?"

"Precisely."

They were still whispering to each other when a tall, thin and slightly stooped man arrived at the entrance of the bar. He glanced around the room, appeared to take note of two men sitting in one corner, walked to a table in the opposite corner and sat down.

"Is that him?" asked Watson.

"Yes. It is. Come, we have to introduce ourselves. I assume you have your service revolver in your pocket."

Chapter Twenty-Six

She's in the Marais

As Holmes and Watson strode over to Oberstein's table, he looked up at them. His deeply-lined face showed the strain of fifteen years as a guest of Her Majesty in an English prison. Suddenly it was altered as expressions first of shock, followed by fear and anger swept over it.

"What in the devil's name are you doing here?" he said.

"A poor way to greet someone you have not seen in nearly twenty years, Mr. Oberstein. And of all the empty bars in all the world, you had to walk into the one in which we were sitting. Such a coincidence would demand sharing a drink together if only the bar were still serving."

"Don't play me for the fool, Holmes. You are not here by chance. That note came from you. So let me tell you that I will have nothing whatsoever to do with you. And let me remind you that I am still a very dangerous man."

With that, he pulled a dagger from his pocket and held it in front of him.

Holmes sighed and rolled his eyes. "Dr. Watson, would you kindly respond?"

Watson took his revolver from his pocket and pointed it at Oberstein. "And let me remind you, sir, that I am still a rather good shot ... well, at least I am from a distance like this."

"Tut, tut, then Mr. Oberstein," said Holmes. "Put that knife of yours away and keep it in your pocket along with the life-preserver that I assume you still always carry with you. We have no interest in exposing you to the French authorities as an agent of the Kaiser. We only wish to come to a mutually beneficial agreement on certain matters."

"What do you want?"

"Three things, all within your power to grant."

"Then speak them."

"First, with regret, you really must leave Paris and return to Germany by way of Geneva tomorrow. It just won't do to have you stay here and work for the downfall of *La République.* Second, you must tell us the names of your contacts. Who is paying you and to whom are you passing along secret data? Those may seem rather inconvenient demands, but when considered in light of the penalty the French are in the habit of administering to spies, they do seem quite reasonable. Would you not agree?"

"That's two. What is the third?"

"You must tell me the location of a certain lady who goes by the name of Mata Hari? You do know her, don't you, and you know where she is?"

Hugo Oberstein gave Holmes an odd look and then laughed. "I might have known that she was behind all this. And now Sherlock Holmes has come running to her rescue. Tell me, Holmes, that she has not bewitched you too."

"Not in the least. I need her for my mission. That is all."

"Oh, yes, of course, you do. But as you are holding all the cards and I value my neck more than my luxurious life here in Paris, I will tell you. Mata Hari is currently residing in the Place des Vosges, number five."

"Thank you, sir. We shall pay her a visit straight away. If you have lied to us, our next visit will be to the office of the French *Deuxièm Bureau,* and they will come looking for you. Now then, I assume she is not living there alone."

"Correct, and neither is she living there by choice. You will need more than a few gold coins to secure her release. Good luck. And if you will excuse me, it appears that I need to pack and find my way to the Gare de Lyon. Give my apologies to the hotel for any balance owing on my account. Good night. I cannot say that it has been a pleasure."

He stood and turned to leave the room.

"One more thing, sir," said Holmes. "The names of your contacts, please."

"All of my country's agents receive our instructions from Gustav Steinhauer in Berlin. But that you could have learned from reading the newspapers. or from Kell and Cumming in London."

"And your contact here to whom you pass documents."

"Another one of our agents, a fanatical Irishman who hates the English. I give you my word on the relics of St. Boniface, I do not know his name and have never wanted to. Gentlemen, *Auf Wiedersehen.*"

He left. Holmes turned to Watson.

"Well, my old friend," said Holmes, "I know it is now past midnight, but we have no choice but to make our move. I recall the Place des Vosges from the days I spent in Paris tracking Huret, the Boulevard assassin. We can walk there."

"How far is it?" asked Watson.

"If my memory serves me correctly, about a half-hour if we move quickly. We need to take a minute to run up to our rooms."

"What for?"

"My gun."

"Fine, but why do I need to come up?"

"Do you have a bottle of chloroform in your medical bag?"

"I always have a small amount."

"Good. Bring it."

LONDON 1887

Chapter Twenty-Seven

The House in the Place des Vosges

26 August, morning

They did not have to walk. Parked on Rue St. Honoré was a large Renault taxi. The driver had sloped back in his seat and was sound asleep. Holmes tapped on the window.

"*Bonjour Mathieu. Réveillez-vous.*"

"*Mon dieu*, what time is it? It cannot be morning already."

"No, but why are you still here? Were you paid to watch us?"

"Non. But now at night there are no fares. *Pas de tout.* So, I tell *moi même* I may as well wait here as drive home. Maybe those two anglos will want a ride in the morning, and *voilà,* here you are."

"Excellent. Kindly take us to Le Marais. Let us out in the Place des Vosges."

"Eh, bien. This I can do. You have a choice of routes. The most direct is past the Bourse, Saint Eustache and Les Halles. At this time of night, we would likely be accosted by a local *gendarme* and detained for driving whilst being sober and therefore looking suspicious. If we cut through the arms of the Louvre, we can drive along the Seine. There you would be seen as yet another couple of men in a taxi with dishonorable intentions and thus ignored."

"The Seine it is then," said Holmes. "The few extra minutes will not matter."

It took more than a few extra minutes owing to Watson's insistence on stopping at the Pont Neuf where he got out of the car. Both banks of the Seine were illuminated by the rows of street lamps that gave their name to the City of Light. The moon was shining clearly, and he could gaze in one direction at the Eiffel Tower and in the other at Notre Dame.

"I really must bring my wife here. There is something quite romantic about this place."

"If you want it to remain as part of France and not annexed by Germany, we cannot afford to dawdle," said Holmes. "Do get back in now."

The hour was approaching one o'clock in the morning when the driver let them off at the Place des Vosges. The open square and gardens were surrounded by shops and residences that had been built over a century ago for wealthy French aristocrats.

"Mathieu," said Holmes, "would you mind waiting for us? I do not expect to be gone long."

The driver grunted his agreement and sloped back down in his seat.

Watson gazed up and down and along the row of elegant connected houses. "Charming place, even in the middle of the night."

"It has been home to some interesting people," said Holmes. "Cardinal Richelieu lived here, as did Victor Hugo. Coincidentally, so did Madame de Sevigné."

"What's coincidental about her?"

"She was a costly courtesan and companion to a long list of rich and powerful men."

"Interesting coincidence. Speaking of which, where is she?"

"Number five. It is directly beside the home once occupied by Victor Hugo. Come, we need to find a way to enter it without being shot."

From a vantage point amongst the trees in the square, they surveyed the front of the house. The large windows on both the first and second were entirely dark. So also were the dormer windows above them. They moved through the arcade and the passage under the first floor into a small courtyard behind the house and again looked up. The windows on the back of the house were likewise dark. There was no sign of anyone being up and around inside, but several of the windows were open to allow the night breeze of late August to flow through.

"Watson," said Holmes, "observe the window on the second floor on the left."

"Yes, what about it?"

"Do you see the dark lines behind the curtains?"

"Yes. I see them. Mullions. Right?"

"Wrong. None of the other windows have the same pattern."

"Right. What of it?"

"They are iron bars, most likely to guard against thieves in a room that housed valuables."

"Fine. What of it?"

"If you wanted to constrain Madam Mata Hari, which room in the house would you keep her in."

"The one with prison bars on the windows, of course. But all that means is that we have to get her out through the door and not the window. Right?"

"This time, correct. I will try the delivery door here in the back. The locks on such doors usually pose no problem. Come, I may need you to light a match so I can see what I am doing."

The moon provided sufficient light for Holmes to find the keyhole in the delivery door. He squatted down, raised his hands and his locksmith tools, and within a minute, he had it open.

Without making a sound except for the inescapable creaking of wooden floorboards in an old home, they moved with deliberate stealth up to the second floor.

"This is the room she must be in," said Holmes, and again he dropped to his knees and silently picked the lock. He gave the handle a slow turn and pushed the door open.

"Can you," he asked Watson, "awake her gently so that she doesn't scream?"

"I think so."

Watson tiptoed to the side of the bed. He lit a match to illuminate the face of the sleeping body that was lying in it. It was Mata Hari. He rocked her shoulder ever so gently and whispered in her ear.

She woke up ... and screamed.

Chapter Twenty-Eight

Inserting a Long, Thick Pin

"Ssshh … madam … it's all right … we're Holmes and Watson … you're safe," Watson whispered in an attempt to calm her. She had seen him in the light from the match and sprang to her knees on the bed.

From the other side of the bed, a man who must have been lying on the floor leapt to his feet. He lunged forward and wrapped his forearm around her neck, pulling her back on the bed.

"Let her go!" shouted Watson. Then the match burned down to his fingers and he threw it aside, sending the room back into darkness.

"Get out of here bloody English," came a voice in the dark. "I have knife. You go now, or I cut her bad."

"You let her go," said Watson. "I have a gun and I will shoot you."

"Fool," came the reply. You cannot see in dark. I have knife. I don't need light. Get out or I cut her."

A light went on. Holmes had flicked the switch on the small lamp on the dresser.

"Now, sir," said Holmes, "we can see you. And you will observe that my friend here has a gun, and it is pointed at you. Let her go."

The assailant shifted his head so that it was almost entirely concealed by Mata Hari's head and luxurious hair. His left arm was around her neck, and he held a dagger in his right. He lowered the tip of the blade until it was touching her breast.

"You want me to cut her? I will. You can shoot me, but she will never dance again. Now go."

Mata Hari flung her hands up to her head and made a vain effort to scratch his eyes. He yanked his head back out of reach, tightened his forearm on her neck, and pushed the tip of the blade against her body until she shrieked with pain. Then she held her body completely still, raised her left hand in front of her body and held up three fingers.

She closed a finger, leaving two. Then she closed another, and then the final one. As she did so, she shot her right hand back behind her body, hitting the man who held her somewhere just below the belt.

He screamed in pain and pulled back from her. She threw herself forward and rolled off the bed and onto the floor.

He dropped the knife and placed both of his hands on his crotch. Watson leapt forward and landed a solid right hook on his jaw. At the same time, Holmes raced to the end of the bed and hit the back of his head with the butt of his gun.

He collapsed on his back onto the bed.

"Your chloroform!" Holmes shouted, and Watson immediately pulled the small bottle from his pocket, opened it and soaked his handkerchief. Before the semi-conscious man could recover, his nose and mouth were covered, and he was soon fully unconscious.

"We need to get out of here," said Holmes, and he started toward the door. "Come, any others will be here in a minute."

Mata Hari was on her feet but was not yet moving. "There are no others. They only leave one guard here at night and the door locked. Another guard comes in the morning, and he is ugly and stupid."

"Madam, half the Place des Vosges heard you scream, and the other half heard him. Get moving."

"I need to get dressed. I am not going to go running around the streets of Paris in my nightgown. I will be ready in five minutes.

"No, madam, now!" said Holmes. "You can get dressed in the taxi."

"Oh, very well, I suppose I can do that. My suitcases are in the closet. If you each take two, I can take two as well."

She picked up the two smallest ones and started out the door and down the stairs. The men followed her, suitcases in hand.

Mathieu loaded five suitcases into the boot of the taxi and Mata Hari, bearing the smallest suitcase, climbed into the seat that was the farthest back in the car. She removed her nightgown, opened the suitcase and started to get dressed.

"*Une femme intéressante* has joined you, I see," said Mathieu. "Where are you taking her?"

"Back to the hotel," said Holmes.

The driver started the car, and they drove along the empty streets of Paris.

"Before you explain how you happened to be held captive, madam," said Holmes, "I must ask, what did you do to that man?"

"I stabbed him with a pin. It is not the first time I have had to do that."

"Your aim was highly accurate."

"It was not difficult, Mr. Holmes. The doctor here will tell you that my chosen target can be found in the same location on every man who ever lived."

"His reaction would suggest you delivered more than a pin prick."

"I keep a long pin in my hair."

"You mean a hair pin?"

"As long as a hairpin, but thicker."

"Would you mind handing it forward so I may have a look at it?"

"I don't have it anymore. I did not pull it out."

"You mean to say that whoever that poor sod was, he is lying unconscious with a long thick pin impaling his—"

"Perhaps," said Watson, interrupting, "we do not need to discuss any further details. We have a picture that is quite clear enough of his condition, and we do not need to imagine his distress when he wakes."

"Right, as always, Watson," said Holmes. "There are some images which make even the toughest of men squirm. Very well then, madam, why were you being held captive in the Place des Vosges?"

"I was kidnapped and was being held for ransom."

Chapter Twenty-Nine

Kidnapped by Whom?

"By whom, madam, were you kidnapped?"

"I don't know their names, but they were all German agents. I was told that I could stay in this lovely house and that seemed like a good arrangement. But when I got there, they locked me up."

"Who sent you there?"

"Hugo Oberstein. That vile miscreant sold me off is what he did."

"Ah, Mr. Oberstein, otherwise known as Mr. Smith, whoever he is. Your words, I believe, madam."

For a moment she was silent, having been caught in a lie. Then she laughed.

"And you believed me when I lied to you? Goodness, Mr. Holmes, what kind of a detective are you?"

She was now fully dressed and leaned forward, extending her head over the back of the seat in front of her. She planted a kiss on the cheek of Sherlock Holmes and laughed again.

"A woman has to do what a woman has to do, sir."

"So, you knew that Oberstein is a German agent?"

"Hugo is an agent of Hugo and no one else. Had you offered to pay him more than the Germans did, he would have worked for you."

"Yet you were foolish enough to trust him."

"He was very generous and pleasant company as long as he did not go on with stories about his time in prison in England."

"What happened between you that he betrayed you?"

"He is getting on a bit. He's almost the same age as you two are and I became bored with him. He did not like my ignoring him, so he convinced one of his associates to kidnap me and demand payment for my safe return."

"From whom?"

"From Georges Ladoux at the *Deuxièm Bureau.*"

"And did he offer to ransom you?"

"No, and I must admit that his lack of interest was rather disappointing. I thought I was valuable to him. But they never heard back from him."

"Did they then try the Germans?"

"Goodness, no. That would have raised far too many questions. So, they sent confidential notices to a few of my wealthiest friends, men whom I considered to care about me."

"As I observed that you were still being held captive, I take it that none of your dear friends was interested in paying a ransom."

She slumped back in her seat and looked out of the taxi window for several seconds before answering.

"No. Not one of them responded. Not one of those men with whom I have spent so many heavenly hours offered a single centime to help me. It appears that I may have outlived my usefulness to them. Do you have a cigarette, Mr. Holmes?"

He offered her one, and she smoked in silence as the taxi cruised along the road beside the Seine.

"Well, madam," said Holmes, "you are still extremely useful to me and Dr. Watson."

"Don't play me for a fool, Mr. Holmes. You may as well be a eunuch and Dr. Watson is happily married. I would not be—"

"Madam, we are not in need of your personal services. We need to send you on yet another mission as a spy."

"Oh, well, that is more interesting. Where to?"

"Berlin."

"And you will pay me if I am successful?"

"Of course. What would you say to three thousand francs?"

"Five and I'll find a way to dance for Kaiser Billy if I have to."

"Five it is."

The taxi had arrived at the hotel and they got out.

"Shall I book you a room?" asked Watson.

"No. I already have a key to one."

"Oh, which room is that?"

"Two-oh-four. I shall see you in the morning."

Chapter Thirty

Going to Berlin

27 August, morning

They met at seven for coffee, croissants and orange juice. Holmes was more specific on the terms of her contract.

"The Germans armies are advancing as we speak across the north of France. The French armies have no specific intelligence as to their strength and vulnerabilities, nor of the routes they have chosen to follow as they descend toward Paris. The British have fewer than one hundred thousand men, and it is impossible for them to stop the Germans by themselves. They held them back at Mons, but the French army on their flank retreated and thus they had to as well. We are not about to send our men to be cannon fodder. If it is impossible to defend Paris, we shall withdraw back across the channel."

"Oh, so you need me to get copies of all of the reports that the generals at the front have been sending back to their superiors in Berlin. Is that right?"

"Right."

"*Bien*, I can do that. It is nothing more than a matter of endearing myself to the appropriate men and getting them to boast—the Germans love to do that to impress a woman—or to steal the most complete recent documents."

"I advise you not to be overconfident. These men are ruthless. They will not hesitate to kill you if you make a mistake and let down your guard."

"If I perish, I perish. Oh, I recall that some other woman has already used that line."

"I believe, my dear lady," said Watson, "that it is from the Bible."

"I know where it is from. She was one of the king's hundred cosseted wives and bedded him to protect her people. What makes her so much more righteous than me if I use the same tactic to save mine?"

The Gare de Lyon was in nearly the same state of disorder and the Gare du Nord. Families, couples, and men and women traveling alone were struggling to board trains to Lyon with the hope of getting out of France and into Switzerland or Italy. Newsagents were hawking the morning papers and shouting about the battle in Le Cateau as if it were an Allied victory when, in truth, it was no more than an effective rear-guard action as the armies retreated.

"I'll get the tickets," said Mata Hari. She slithered her way through the pandemonium and returned ten minutes later with three first-class tickets to Lyons.

"I would have preferred my own private cabin, but those are not to be had. It will be necessary for us to sit together along with three other people. Under the circumstances, it will just have to be endured."

They boarded the next train to take them south to Lyon, where they would change for a train across the border into Switzerland.

Geneva was their final destination. The journey would take them all day. It was late afternoon by the time their train arrived at the Cornavin station in Geneva.

"My favorite hotel here is the Beau Rivage," said Mata Hari. "It is only a few blocks away. You will like it. Follow me."

"Madam," said Holmes, "you are not going there."

"Why not? The food is good, the view is heavenly."

"Because, madam, you are going directly to Berlin. The German armies are less than a week away from Paris. We do not have time for you to spend a night in Geneva. We cannot cross the border. You can. You will have to leave now and take an overnight train to Berlin. Kindly buy yourself a sleeper cabin and try to get some rest. You will need it."

She was not happy and made her feelings known in a few choice words, but she bought herself a ticket to Berlin.

"And where am I supposed to find you two when I get back here?"

"In the Beau Rivage. It has been highly recommended."

From the station, she sent a telegram to the German cabinet minister she thought might be her most advantageous source of information. An hour later, an answer came back confirming that he would be pleased to meet her the following evening to receive her report.

Having secured that meeting, she then sent another telegram to Alfred Kiepert, a German army officer and one of her dear friends from her first performances in Vienna and Berlin a decade earlier. She knew that, as always, he would be thrilled to spend a few hours with her as long as his wife did not intercept the message.

Her train arrived at the border with Germany at eight o'clock that night, and she was questioned by the German border guards. She answered all of their questions in fluent German and an affected case of French ennui.

"Frau Zelle, you must tell us to whom in Berlin you are paying a visit."

"Oh, very well, if you insist on knowing. His name is Herr Gottlieb von Jagow. He is your Secretary of State for Foreign Affairs and a dear friend. Here is the telegram confirming our meeting tomorrow. Now, kindly move on and bother the other passengers."

Chapter Thirty-One

Useful Former Lovers

Her train arrived at the Berlin Central Station twelve hours later. Unlike the train stations in France, this one was running in perfect order. Trains were arriving and leaving on time, as they always did in Germany.

An elegant Benz taxicab took her to the Aldon Hotel on the other side of the Spree River. It was one of the best in the city and only a block or two from the Reichstag and the offices of the ministers of the German government.

"Welcome, Mata Hari," said the beaming hotel clerk. "Once again you grace us with your patronage."

"So good to see you as well, Hans. With your blond hair and blue eyes, you are such a treat to look at. Such a shame that you're not rich."

The clerk laughed. "Some day, my dear goddess. Your usual suite, madam?"

"*Bitte,* and nothing to disturb me until noon. I will be sleeping."

Before going up to her room, she went to the breakfast room in the hope of enjoying a coffee and strudel before napping. At the door of the room, she froze. Seated on the far side was Hugo Oberstein. He was reading a newspaper and sipping a coffee and did not see her. She turned around immediately and went to her room.

"That *kruipen*," she muttered to herself. "He sells me out and now ruins my breakfast. No man does that to Mata Hari."

When she first met Albert Kiepert he was a wealthy young lieutenant and charming *bon vivant* and held a post in the prestigious *Krefelder Tanzhusaren,* an elite Hussar unit in the Royal Prussian Army. He had kept her sumptuously during those halcyon days and, over a decade later, he was a major and, as fortune would have it, stationed in Berlin and working for Erich Ludendorff, the quartermaster general. They spent a splendid two hours that afternoon becoming reacquainted. She listened patiently as he enjoyed a post-meeting cigarette and generous glass of Jägermeister and complained about the enormous problems he was facing getting adequate food, potable water, medicines and ammunition to the men on the western front.

"And forage for the horses," he said. "You would not believe how hard it is to feed tens of thousands of horses when they are hundreds of miles away. Those French *Schweine* are destroying their bridges and railways as they run from us."

She listened with great sympathy and offered a few sensible suggestions that elicited more detailed complaining from the major. Then, with a warm kiss, she sent him back to his office and his wife and pocketed the money he left behind. To his credit, he left her gold marks even though they had been replaced a few days earlier with the *papiermarks* that were already falling in value.

She would have to keep in contact with him once the war was over.

To avoid running into Oberstein, whom she cursed one more time, she had an early supper sent up to her room. By seven o'clock she was ready to meet her primary target and took a taxi to the Potsdamer Platz and knocked on the door of the stately residence of the German minister of foreign affairs. A pretty young *Fräulein* greeted her and led her to the office and library. As they walked down the hall, the maid looked up at Mata Hari and whispered.

"*Du bist meine Heldin,* Mata Hari. I dream that I could be like you."

"*Mein Schatz,* be good to all the rich men who pass through this door, and you will have no worries ever."

When she entered the library, three men stood to greet her. She had expected to meet with Gottlieb von Jagow, but standing in front of her were also Major Walter Nicolai of the German intelligence services and, to her profound surprise, the chancellor himself, Theobald von Bethmann Hollweg.

"Good evening, Frau Zelle," said the minister. "Or may I call you our H21? I informed Major Nicolai of my plan to meet with you. He insisted on being present and informed the chancellor. As you see, he has honored us with his presence."

For a moment, she trembled ever so slightly with intimidation, but then she used a tactic that had proven useful in the past when meeting with powerful men. She imagined the three of them standing in front of her *sans vêtements* and then, with their protruding tummies and sagging chests, they were just three more men. And men were easy.

"A glass of Riesling, madam?" asked the minister.

"*Danke schön* but no, Herr von Jagow. Herr Kroemer made it clear to me that I must have a perfectly clear head when giving you my report."

"Ah, yes, Kroemer, by the book. Right, well forgive us if we do not follow his instructions as you tell us what you learned about the operations of the French and British whilst you were living in Paris."

"What I learned, gentlemen, is that the war is almost over. The French and British are marching back to Paris as fast as their little legs will carry them. The French put all their eggs in the basket of trying to recapture Alsace, and you drove them back. They are crushed. The British are not prepared to lose any more men to protect the French. Their leader, Marshall French, is ready to take his men home."

"Ah, that is good to know," said the chancellor. "Have they heard about our victories over the Russians?"

"Oh, yes sir, they have. It was not good news for them. Now they are terrified of General Hindenburg. The French were relying on the Russians to keep marching into Prussia and were crying into their absinthe when they heard about the Battle near Tannenberg."

For the next hour, she answered their questions, making use of some data that were supposed to be secret, some that were available from any newspaper, and some that she made up. She was careful to request clarification of their questions and, in doing so, acquired useful intelligence concerning the advance toward Paris on the western front.

"Do tell me," she said, "how my good friends the Crown Prince and Duke Rupert are getting along. Are their 5th and 6th armies holding up for them?"

She had been blessed with an excellent memory and had learned how important it was to remember details. Usually those details consisted of the dates of birthdays, the names of wives and children, and any peculiar activities that brought pleasure.

They thanked her and were about to call the maid to see her out when she gave them an imploring look.

"There is something else you should be aware of, and it embarrasses me to have to tell you, for I was also tricked by a most vile man." She lowered her gaze and looked at the floor, and then added. "I confess, I was in love with him."

"Who are you talking about?" demanded Major Nicolai.

"His name is Herr Hugo Oberstein. I assume you know him."

"Ya, we know him. What about him?"

"He's a traitor. I gave him the documents that Karl Kroemer had entrusted to me, and he handed them off immediately to a British agent. He is taking money from all sides in this conflict."

"We shall deal with him accordingly," said the major. "We thank you for bringing this to our attention even if it was difficult to do so."

As soon as she was dismissed along with the grateful thanks and praise of the men to whom she had made her report, she rushed back to her hotel and wrote down everything they had said.

She had one more day in Berlin to learn all she could and who better than former lovers to meet and talk to. She sent notes off to Captain Runtze, commander of the naval base at Seefliegerhorst, and to Herr Griebel, the Chief of Police in Berlin. They too would know things.

Chapter Thirty-Two

Trading Places

The twenty-ninth of August was a glorious summer Saturday in Berlin, and Mata Hari looked forward to dividing her time between two of her dear friends whom she had not seen for several years.

A note arrived at the hotel from Herr Griebel, the Chief of Police. She eagerly opened the envelope only to read:

As you are a foreign national and Germany is at war, it is not appropriate for me to meet with you.

"It is not as if I am the enemy," she complained to the mirror in her room. "He might have at least expressed his regrets and said something about all those wonderful days we spent together. It was not all that long ago."

A telegram arrived soon afterward from Captain Runtze. He was stationed at the naval base and was a full day's travel from

Berlin. He graciously referred back to the wonderful times they had shared and said that he deeply regretted not being able to meet with her.

"That was decent of him," she thought. "of course, he was always happy to meet with any woman who was not his jealous Hungarian wife."

Her ticket was for the overnight train back to Geneva, so she would not be able to leave Berlin until the evening. She would have to spend her last day in Berlin alone.

Unlike Paris, where panic about the encroaching war had pervaded the city, Berlin was quiet, even peaceful. It was a beautiful August day, and she took advantage of her free time to stroll through one of her favorite cities. The rhododendrons and the roses were in full bloom in their respective plots in the Tiergarten, and the young couples were walking hand in hand as if they were safe forever from the carnage of the war. She remembered the walks she had enjoyed with various dear friends and wished that the war would end soon so she could resume her joyful outings.

She wandered past the opera house and recalled her performances there when every seat in the hall was filled, and her fans, both men and women, applauded loud and long and threw roses onto the stage. The island in the Spree had been another of her favorite places, and she stopped briefly to sit inside the Berlin Cathedral. Piety, however, was not one of her dominant characteristics, and she did not stay long. Then she looked in at the continuing construction of the Pergamon Museum. If the rumors were to be believed, some crafty German archeologist had managed to steal the entire Walls of Babylon from excavations in Persia. They would soon be mounted in the museum for all of Europe to enjoy.

When she returned to the Aldon Hotel at the end of the afternoon, she casually asked at the front desk if a Mr. Oberstein was still a guest.

"No, madam," the clerk told her. "He departed this morning."

"Oh, what a surprise. He seemed to be enjoying his stay here."

"He was. His departure came as a surprise to him as well, if you know what I mean."

"I am not sure I do, but if he returns, do give him my greetings."

"I shall, madam. And he left a message for you. It is in your box."

He handed Mata Hari a small envelope. In it was a note that read: *Schlampe.* I will repay you."

"*Scheisse,*" she said to herself and hurried up to her room to pack.

With all of her notes stuffed into her handbag, she hurried to the Central station to board the overnight train back to Geneva. Several times, she was sure that the man she saw following her was Hugo Oberstein, but it proved to be only another middle-aged German who bore the same hat, coat, and shape as Oberstein. At nine o'clock on the evening of 29 August, she breathed a sigh of relief as her train departed. There were no sleeper cabins on this run, and she would have to remain in her seat throughout the night.

The train stopped numerous times as it made its way south. There were over a dozen whistle stops and longer delays at Hanover, Frankfurt and Mannheim. At each of the longer stops, German officials boarded the train and checked the papers of every passenger.

It was around two o'clock in the morning when the train stopped in Frankfurt, and she got out with the hope of finding a café open at that hour. Except for a handful of passengers getting on and off the train, the cavernous station was empty. As she walked along the platform, she heard the footsteps of someone close behind her and casually turned her head to see who it was.

She recognized him.

He was one of the thugs Oberstein and his associates had hired to guard her in the Place des Vosges, the ugly and stupid one. He waved to her and fear swept over her entire body. She changed her direction and walked smartly toward the women's lavatory.

Once inside, she noticed another woman, a passenger who, like herself, had preferred the spacious and gleaming clean facilities offered by the station to the cramped toilet cubicle on the train. The woman looked about the same age as Mata Hari and was also tall with a light brown hue to her skin color. Mata Hari looked at her … and had an idea.

"Are you on your way to Geneva as well?" she asked. "What is taking you there?"

"I have been accepted as a governess to a Swiss family. What about you?"

"I am meeting a man who wants to marry me."

"Oh, you must be quite excited."

"No, in truth I am very upset, and I don't know what to do about it."

"Oh no, what is wrong?"

"He says he loves me, but I fear that all he is interested in is my family's money."

"Oh, yes, men are like that, aren't they? Is there any way you can put him to the test so you will know for certain?"

Mata Hari affected distress and shook her head. "I am at a loss. I cannot think of anything … or maybe I can." She was now smiling at the other woman.

"Oh my, tell me."

"These clothes I am wearing. They mark me as a wealthy woman, do they not?"

"Why, of course they do. Your suit is beautifully tailored and of the finest quality. Your boots and hat must have cost a fortune. Yes, of course, you appear to come from a rich family."

"It is madness to ask, but would you … could you consider changing clothes with me? You are dressed very smartly, but your costume is appropriate for a governess. We are the same size and height. Then when I meet this man, he will think that I am not

166

wealthy at all. If he still professes love for me, I will know. Oh, no, that was silly of me to make such a request. I'm so sorry. Please ignore—"

"Oh no, not at all. It is a good idea. It will be fun to see what happens. We can meet in a few days in Geneva and change back."

"Would you truly do that? Oh, thank you. And do not worry about getting my clothes back to me. You can keep them, or sell them, or do whatever you want with them. It is I who will be in your debt."

The two of them quickly changed their clothes, laughing and giggling about the foibles and foolishness of the male species.

"And here," said Mata Hari. "You must take my ticket and sit in my seat in first-class. Otherwise the conductors will start to wonder."

"Oh no. I am back in the third-class. You would not be comfortable."

"Nonsense. It is only a few more hours until we reach Geneva."

"That is so kind and generous of you. By the way, my name is Agathe. Aggie."

"Mine is Margaretha. M'greet. It has been lovely to meet you. And thank you again for helping me. I am very grateful, Aggie."

The governess left the lavatory first, dressed elegantly, and walked regally toward the first-class car. Mata Hari waited a minute and then walked, somewhat slouched, toward the third-class cars. The man she recognized appeared from behind a newsagent's stand and followed the governess.

Chapter Thirty-Three

She is My Friend

Sitting upright in the third-class car, along with screaming children and snoring old men and women from all corners of the continent, was not Mata Hari's preferred mode of travel. Nevertheless, she could do what was necessary for a few hours as long as there awaited a fine hotel and a financial reward at the end of the journey.

It was still five hours to Geneva, and it could be longer if they were delayed at the border. For a moment, she panicked, thinking that she should have exchanged passports with Agathe, but it was too late for that now.

The final obstacle was the border with Switzerland. It was not likely that the Swiss would check passports very closely as they did not seem to care who entered the country as long as they brought money with them. Governesses were always welcome in every country in Europe as wealthy parents always thought they were doing a favor for their children by contracting a woman from another country and language to be their teacher.

At six o'clock in the morning, the train stopped at the border in the northern extension of Basel. Bored border guards entered the train and instructed the passengers to hold up their passports.

Without looking up at them, Mata Hari held hers up. The name *Mata Hari,* of course, did not appear in it. To the young Swiss border guard, the name of Margaretha Zelle MacLeod in a Dutch passport meant nothing. He glanced at it and moved on.

The guards walked down the corridors nodding to the seats on both sides of the aisle as they passed and moved on to the next railway car. Ten minutes later, the train started up again and proceeded through the early morning light and on its way through Basel.

It stopped again for ten minutes each in Bern and Lausanne and in a dozen Swiss towns, but no Swiss police or government agents appeared. Three hours later, it arrived at the Cornavin station. Mata Hari stepped off and moved quickly to a spot beside a newsagent's stand where she could observe the other passengers. She needed to see if the man who had been following her continued to follow Agathe.

She saw him. He moved along the platform with a cluster of other passengers and headed toward the front door of the station. He was not following Agathe. That was good. But then the line of passengers from the first-class car ended with no sign of Agathe.

One of the train staff leapt off the car and blew hard on a whistle. A policeman ran toward him, and the two of them stepped back onto the car. A minute later, the policeman came back out and ran to a telephone. He then stood in the entryway of the station and stared out the door.

An ambulance arrived, its bell clanging, and two attendants jumped out and ran toward the rail car. One of them was carrying a canvas stretcher. They emerged soon after holding the stretcher at both ends and tilting it sharply so that it could be lowered from the

169

train to the platform. A sheet was draped over the top of it. The contour of a body underneath the sheet was unmistakable. The attendants turned and started walking toward the station entrance. Mata Hari ran after them.

She caught up to them and pulled back the sheet covering the body. The lifeless eyes of Agathe stared up at her. A fur collar and a beautiful embroidered jacket framed her face.

"Madam," shouted one of the attendants. "Get away. Do not do that. Stop it. Now!"

"This woman," she said, "is my friend. What happened to her?"

"We do not know. If you are her friend, then come to the hospital with us and help identify her."

She followed them to the ambulance but did not get in. She turned away at the last minute, joined a group of the passengers who were along the pavement, and plodded very slowly toward the Beau Rivage Hotel.

Chapter Thirty-Four

Attacked in Geneva

On the evening of 29 August, two days before Mata Hari's return to Geneva, Holmes and Watson sat on the terrace of the Beau Rivage Hotel, enjoying the tranquil view over Lake Geneva. It was a balmy summer evening, and the two of them had abandoned their formal traveling clothes for more casual wear.

"You are putting a rather large amount of faith in her, are you not?" said Watson.

"If there were any other course of action open to me, I would take it. But the data we want are in Berlin, and we cannot go there. She can. She is our only option."

"What's to stop her from deciding to stay in Berlin. Goodness knows, she has enough dear friends amongst the German generals and politicians."

"Money. I offered her another five hundred francs if she could return by Sunday with the intelligence we need. And we need it desperately if the German advance is to be stopped. As you know, I am not a man who is given to prayer, but I may have uttered one or two short orisons to the Almighty beseeching her soon and safe return."

"I would be tempted," said Watson, "to do likewise if it were not for the fact that I am certain that the faithful in Germany are also invoking divine intervention for their side."

Holmes said nothing but made murmuring sounds of agreement. They ordered a second round of schnaps and sipped in silence for the better part of an hour.

"Watson," said Holmes, "do not look now, but on our left, there is a man sitting on the balcony of his room, and he has been glancing in all directions for some time now. A minute ago, he retreated to his room and returned with a set of field glasses."

"Are there any attractive women still splashing in the hotel pool? The Swiss do have a reputation for ogling, you know. Not as bad as the Americans but nonetheless—"

"He has now fixed his gaze on us, and I assure you that no one, not even a drunken Russian, would mistake either you or me for an attractive young woman."

"Speak for yourself, Holmes," said Watson and then he laughed loudly, his sense of humor having been badly altered by one schnaps too many.

"The thought of his leering at you, my dear doctor, gives a whole new meaning to the sin of indecent behavior. Come, time to retire for the night before you engender any more impure leering looks upon your sagging frame. You do still have your service revolver in your pocket, do you not?"

"I do. Are you now suggesting that I might need it to defend myself against this depraved voyeur?"

"One must always be prepared to protect one's virtue, and as his room is on the same floor in the same wing as ours, one should be ready for all possible eventualities. Oh, and would you mind bringing the bottle of that sickly sweet liqueur and snifters with you. A final round would help to soothe my worries."

"Ah ha, about her?"

"Certainly not about you."

They entered Holmes's room, sat in the comfortable armchairs and poured themselves another round. They were about to imbibe when the door to the room's private lavatory opened and a man emerged. He was carrying a gun and pointing it directly at them.

"Do not move," he said.

Holmes immediately stood up, turned to face him and raised his hands. Watson did likewise.

"I said don't move!"

"How terribly ill-mannered you are, old chap," said Holmes. "Here I thought that German men prided themselves on their fine manners and social graces."

As he spoke, he moved a foot or two to one side so that his body was now directly in line with Watson's and blocking the view this unknown assailant had of Watson.

"Are you crazy!? I said, don't move. Now go back to where you were or I will shoot."

"Oh, dear me," said Holmes. "So terribly sorry. It must have been all that dreadful schnaps. So sorry, I did not understand your wishes."

He stepped aside, and the intruder found himself facing Watson directly. The only difference was that Watson now had his service revolver in hand and was pointing it directly at the German.

For a moment, the assailant looked befuddled by the turn of events. Although it had been nearly four decades since Dr. John Watson had served with the Fifth Northumberland Fusiliers, there was one lesson that he had not forgotten, schnaps notwithstanding. That being, if two enemies are pointing guns at each other, the one who does not elect to fire first is invariably the loser.

He shot the man in the leg.

He screamed in pain and fell back onto the floor. Holmes was on him in a flash and took the gun away. He had no sooner done that than Watson had one knee on the fellow's chest and a revolver pointed at his head.

The face of the man on the floor had lost its color from the effect of pain and fear.

"*Bitte, bitte,* do not shoot me. I am only doing what I was paid to do."

"Were you now?" said Holmes. "By whom?"

"I do not know his name, I swear."

"Oh my, that is unfortunate. Watson, would you mind putting a bullet into his other leg. Perhaps it will improve his memory."

Watson slowly drew the barrel of his revolver down across the man's throat and then down his chest and stomach.

"Perhaps here would be better than in his leg." He said as he pointed the gun directly at a vulnerable place on the body a few inches below the abdomen. "I suspect that the mere threat of a bullet in this part of the anatomy would be even more useful in improving his memory."

The look on the man's face now descended from fear to wide-eyed terror.

"No! No, I beg you. I do not know his name. He was not one of us. He was one of you. He was English."

"What?" said Holmes. "Are you saying that an Englishman ordered you to kill us?"

"No. No. Not to kill you. Only to force you into a room in the basement and keep you there until this woman, this Mata Hari returned. Then I could let you go."

"That sounds like nonsense to me," said Holmes. "You imprison us, and then as soon as Mata Hari appears, you let us go."

"No. No. He said wait for two hours. That was all he would need with her. Then let you go. That is what he said. I swear it was."

"Describe this man."

"It was dark, he—"

"Watson, perhaps a small push of your revolver against a tender part of his body would be in order as a prelude to a bullet."

Watson complied and pushed the barrel of his gun directly into the chap's nether region. He howled in pain.

"He was tall. That's all I can tell you. Broad-shouldered. I could not see his face."

"How did he know you? Do not tell me it was dark, or you will be shot."

"I work for Oberstein. He recommended me."

"Ah, now that does sound credible. Watson, is your handy little bottle in your other pocket?"

"It is."

"Good. Keep the gun pointed where it is and use it if necessary. And you, sir, are about to have a short nap. Do not worry. When you wake up, there will be a pretty Swiss miss in a nurse's uniform to look after you."

Holmes extracted the bottle of chloroform from Watson's pocket, soaked his handkerchief and held it against the nose and mouth. The man on the floor, apparently knowing that becoming unconscious was to be preferred to the alternative, did not put up a struggle. He was unconscious within less than a minute.

"Now what are you going to do with him?" asked Watson.

Chapter Thirty-Five

I Don't Know Who I Am

"Is he in danger from the wound?" asked Holmes.

"No. I aimed for his *vastus medialis*. There are no arteries near it. A tight bandage will stop the bleeding."

"A surprising good aim, my old friend. After the schnaps, I feared you would be seeing double."

"That common situation was covered during basic training. When seeing two enemies, close one eye and aim. It still works but does not solve the problem of how to get rid of him before the police arrive."

"Is our room not situated directly above the hotel kitchen?" asked Holmes

"I believe it is."

"Excellent. Wait here."

Holmes reappeared a few minutes later, pushing a food cart usually used for delivering substantial orders of room service. The lower tray was covered by a skirt that they unpinned, allowing them to stuff and tie the unconscious body of their would-be kidnapper onto the cart. A note was affixed to the top telling the recipient, in German, *Take me to the hospital.*

They wheeled the cart down the hall to the lift and pressed the button to call for it. Then they hurried back to their room as if they were naughty schoolboys who knocked on the doors of a unliked neighbor and ran away.

"And now what happens?" said Watson.

"Unless we are threatened again, we wait here for Mata Hari to come to us. Pray, she will do so soon."

The entire next day passed and she did not appear. On the morning of 30 August, she arrived, her complexion completely drained of color and her lower lip trembling.

"Merciful heavens, my dear," said Watson. "You look like you've seen a ghost."

"I have, Doctor. Mine. A few minutes ago, I looked upon myself … dead."

Watson had her sit down in his room and called for Holmes. After a brandy and a cigarette, she told her story and her final look at the body of the friendly governess.

"You are understandably shaken, madam, and have our deepest sympathies," said Holmes. "Now then, were you able to secure the data we need?

She nodded and retrieved her notes.

"You will not be able to understand them," she said. "I was careful not to write anything that could reveal what I learned to anyone else. They only contain words and numbers to jog my memory. Everything you need to know is inside my head."

"Excellent, madam. Then best we go straight away to the station and be on our way back to Paris."

"Do we have to go now? Can I not have an hour or two to rest and put my soul back together?"

"With regret, madam—"

"Yes, my dear, of course we can," said Watson. "We have already missed the early morning train to Lyons. The next one does not leave for another hour. Holmes and I will leave you in my room, and I suggest that you take a long nap."

"Thank you, Doctor. You are a kind man. But no, I will not be able to sleep. I am too … too … I don't know what I am. I would like to go for a walk by myself through the gardens and along the quai … and gaze across the water and up to Mont Blanc. That is what I need."

"Of course, you can," said Watson.

"But not by yourself," said Holmes. "Whoever thought they killed you is at large in this city. Doctor Watson and I shall follow you at a distance to ensure your safety."

"I will also need to visit one of the shops nearby. I cannot be seen in Paris dressed like a governess."

After another brandy and cigarette, Mata Hari departed the hotel and stood for several minutes beside the Quai du Mont Blanc and gazed over the lake and up to the mountains. The hour was still early, and although a few motorcars and lorries were moving along the road, no other pedestrians were yet strolling along the seawall or in the gardens. She turned to her right, entered the Square des Bergues and wandered through its beds of alpine flowers.

In the center of the square was the mausoleum monument to the Duke of Brunswick, the great benefactor of the city of Geneva. It was a three-story-tall ornate structure made entirely of white Carrara marble. It housed the sarcophagus and the duke's remains, enclosed in a hexagon of marble walls. The front wall, facing the waters of Lake Geneva, had an opening, allowing the public to enter and contemplate the statuary and bas-relief and the supine carved likeness of the duke.

Perhaps Mata Hari thought that looking upon the final resting place of an exceptionally rich man might bring some sense of peace and meaning to her life. We shall never know. For as soon as she entered the enclosure, two men emerged from behind the walls and grabbed her by her arms. Both were armed with pistols and held them firmly against her torso.

She screamed and Holmes and Watson came running toward her.

"Do not try anything!" shouted one of her assailants. "If you take out your revolvers, she will be shot dead."

The two men forced Mata Hari out of the mausoleum and down the steps.

"You! Holmes and Watson! Walk in front of us. Go straight ahead toward the boats. Move or we will shoot."

Holmes and Watson, seeing no alternative, submitted and walked slowly through the square, past the Brunswick Lions and across to the edge of the lake. A row of small fishing and pleasure boats was tied up against the seawall, separated by short, individual piers.

"The pier on your left! Then step into the boat on the right!"

The boat was a small fishing craft about twenty-five feet long. The back portion of the deck was full of nets and fishing gear. A short set of stairs adjacent to the helm led down into a cabin.

"Stand in front of those stairs," came the order.

"Now you, Mata Hari. Stand beside them."

She did as she was told, and the three of them formed a short line, looking up at the men who were standing on the pier with their guns pointed at them.

"*Mon dieu,*" screamed Mata Hari. "They are going to kill us."

The men raised their guns. One was pointed at Holmes and the other at Mata Hari.

"Only you and Sherlock Holmes," said one of them. "You are spies. Doctor Watson can write about your execution."

Mata Hari made a quick gesture approximating the sign of the cross against her body. Sherlock Holmes smiled serenely at the men who were about to kill him.

Two shots exploded in the early morning stillness.

Neither Holmes nor Mata Hari moved. The would-be executioners toppled forward into the boat and pools of blood immediately appeared beside their heads. A man bearing a Luger pistol emerged from the boat berthed next to the one they were in and climbed up onto the pier.

"We really must stop meeting like this," said Lieutenant O'Hara. "Come quickly, please. I have a car waiting. I'll get us to the station, but we will not be able to return to the hotel. That would be a bit too risky."

"Thank you, Lieutenant," said Holmes. "But would you mind terribly—"

"I will on the train," O'Hara replied.

He led them to a parked motorcar, and he sat in the driver's seat. They pulled away from the quai, and he turned into the heart of the city and toward the Geneva train station.

"Would it be possible," asked Mata Hari, "to stop at one of the shops along this street? As I am still alive, I need to treat myself to a new frock and stole to wear when we arrive in Paris."

In unison, all three men replied.

"NO."

Chapter Thirty-Six

Blood is Thicker Than Water

Ninety minutes later, the train stopped at the border with France. A French military officer opened their cabin door and demanded to be shown their papers. Lieutenant O'Hara handed over his passport along with a document that appeared to bear two rather official-looking stamps. The French private formed his lips into a duckbill, nodded, and returned the papers.

"*Bienvenue en France, mes amis*" he said and moved on to the next cabin.

As the train crossed the border and entered France, Holmes demanded an explanation.

"As this is the second time, Lieutenant O'Hara, that you have interrupted our being murdered, I do believe that some explanation is in order."

"Perfectly understandable. What would you like to know?"

"To start with, who are you working for?"

"Ah, yes, let me see. Well, there's an office somewhere in Whitehall that cannot be named. That's number one. Then there's the *Deuxième Bureau* in Paris. And poor old Hugo Oberstein thinks I'm working for him as well."

"And which of them commands your true loyalty?"

"None. My only allegiance is to Ireland and the Irish Volunteers."

"Knowing that does not help me at all to understand why you have reappeared and saved our lives. Your story, please, sir. Or are you bound to secrecy?"

"On some matters, yes. Others, no. I will tell you what I can, and I assure you that at least one-half of what I tell you will be God's truth."

"Half a loaf is better than none. Proceed."

"It seems that someone in the Admiralty was told that I was a fairly bright chap and had the capacity for naval intelligence work. After working in the branch for a year or so, I was tapped for special services, about which I cannot say anything."

"Then continue with what you can say."

"Sooo ... I may have grown up in Yorkshire, but my family roots are deep into Sligo, and I cannot deny that I am a loyal son of the sod and a firm believer in Home Rule. That became a problem for me."

"The Home Rule Act was passed. There is nothing illegal in supporting the cause," said Holmes.

"True, Mr. Holmes, but I was made aware that the Germans had offered to send twenty-thousand rifles and half-a-million rounds of ammunition to the Irish Volunteers should we have to take up arms against the Ulster Volunteers and the British Army. If it came to a shooting war, I would have no choice but to join with the Irish Republican Brotherhood and take up arms. But that was all put aside when war was declared."

"And up until that time, you were spying on the British for the Irish?"

"You might put it that way. I let one of the brothers know that you and Dr. Watson were being sent to France as spies and another one of the brothers passed that along to his friends in Germany who were offering the rifles. He then sent that fellow to shoot you in the lavatory of the ferry. I had been assigned by Whitehall to follow you and guard you, and so I had to shoot the German."

"Fine. But that does not yet explain your presence here this morning."

"Oh, that, well, I was then sent to offer my services to Hugo Oberstein in Paris. Undercover, of course. I claimed to be a zealot for the Irish cause and so angry at the English that I would be thrilled to have them defeated by the Germans. He, as I am sure you can understand, does not like the English, and he does not like you at all, Mr. Holmes and has been of that opinion since you helped send him away for fifteen years."

"He received his just deserts. Bearing a grudge is not a wise thing to do. It invariably leads to one's own demise."

"If you say so, sir. However, he was also terribly angry at you, madam. He is now sitting in a French prison cell, thanks to you. So he sent me along with several other of his associates to follow you. One of them murdered that poor woman on the train with whom you changed clothes. The rest of us followed you to the hotel in Geneva, where we discovered Mr. Holmes and Dr. Watson. I was over-ruled, and the others decided that you would have to die not only for your betrayal of Oberstein, but for your spying against Germany. As soon as the three of you left the hotel this morning, two of those men hid in the monument, and two others took up places along the promenade. I looked around and asked myself, if I were a killer, where would I take my victims before shooting them. The boats on the other side of the road were the obvious choice. So, I went there."

"Why have you changed sides?" asked Holmes.

"I haven't. But war was declared. Several thousand young Irish lads ignored their religion and immediately signed up to fight. Tens of thousands more are doing so as we speak. I have cousins by the score in both Sligo and Antrim who have volunteered to fight the Germans. I was not about to do nothing as the Germans slaughtered them. The movement for independence and unrestricted Home Rule had to be put aside. Blood, sir, is thicker not only than water but also than politics or even religion. And if push came to shove, we Irish would rather be still speaking English ten years for now than German. So, here I am. And that is the end of my story ... for now.

"Are you joining us in Paris to deliver our report?"

"No, I fear not. I will bid you goodbye in Lyon. You will be safe from there, and my next assignment is waiting for me."

"And will it involve protecting any more English spies and shooting Germans?"

"That I cannot say. Another secret. Well, I suppose I could tell you, but then I would have to shoot you."

At the station in Lyon, he vanished into the crowd of French people who were fleeing the war.

Chapter Thirty-Seven

Delivering the Data

Throughout the remainder of the day, they traveled north to Paris. The train was almost empty. Everyone in France had heard the news. The massive German army was within three or four days of Paris. The French army continued to retreat. It was a repeat of the war of 1870, except this time it was happening more rapidly than anyone could have imagined.

Holmes, Watson and Mata Hari sat in silence, occasionally catching a nap as they rolled on through Bourgogne and Ile-de-France. When they were within a half-hour of the Gare de Lyon, Holmes insisted on a complete review of the data Mara Hari had acquired.

"Very well done, madam. You see and you also observe. Your memory is brilliant."

"I am so happy you think so, sir. Does that mean that you will be able to impart everything to whoever you have to talk to without my being there?"

"No."

"Why not?"

"They will wish to confirm the accuracy of what we tell them and will ask very specific questions that only you can answer. Be prepared. We meet in the Quai d'Orsay first thing tomorrow morning."

"Fine. Where are we staying tonight?"

"The Hotel du Louvre."

"*Merveilleux.* All my belongings are there. I will not have to go out to Rue Saint Honoré to buy more clothes before the meeting."

"Honestly, madam, is that all you ever think about?"

"Not at all. I am thinking about the men who will be at the meeting. They will be men who have power and money. What do you think about?"

The sun had set by the time they arrived in Paris, and they took a taxi immediately to the hotel. They ate dinner in their rooms and slept.

On the following morning, the first day of September 1914, they found Mathieu the taxi driver still waiting outside the hotel on the Rue de Rivoli.

"*Sacré bleu.* You are still here ... and you are alive. Where do you want to go? The *boche* is almost on our doorstep."

"The Quai d'Orsay," said Holmes.

"*Zut alors,* I knew you must be spies. You best go there and then get out of Paris as fast as you can. Those Germans, they like to shoot spies, *vous le savez*?"

"We have become aware of that."

A French sergeant met them at the door of Number 37 Quai d'Orsay, and led them inside. On the top floor, another officer escorted them to a massive office decorated with paintings and busts of Napoleon and adorned with a large window that afforded a superb view of the Seine.

"Please be seated," said the officer. "The men will be with you in a few minutes. Kindly be prepared to deliver what you have to say within fifteen minutes. They are very busy."

Ten minutes later, four men entered the room. Holmes and Watson recognized all of them. General Joseph Joffre, the Commander-in-Chief of the French forces led the way. Lord Kitchener, the British Secretary of State for War, followed him, as did Sir John French, the commander of the BEF. The last to enter was General Joseph Gallieni, the military governor of Paris.

"Mr. Holmes," said Lord Kitchener, "we must decide by the end of the day today whether to withdraw the BEF to England. General Joffre may have to abandon Paris to the Germans. What news can you bring to us that is pertinent to our situation? Please be precise and concise."

"The data provided to me lead to only one conclusion. We should not only stand and fight. We will also have to opportunity to counter-attack and drive the Germans back toward Belgium."

"Go on," said Kitchener.

"The salient points are as follows. Even though the Germans were able to inflict horrible losses on the French army along the frontier, they have lost far more men than we have. The action by the Belgian army and the BEF at Mons and Le Cateau impeded their advance. The primary result is that it has given the Russians more time to attack in the east, and thus the Kaiser has been forced to send over one hundred thousand soldiers from the western front to the eastern. They are winning the battles over there, but in doing so they have reduced their western forces."

"That still leaves them with over half-a-million pouring down on us from the north," said Kitchener.

"Correct, sir. However, we have learned that their men have been forced to march over one hundred and fifty miles with no more than a few hours sleep at night. They are exhausted and will not be ready for battle without a day or two of rest. Most are young recruits and not used to the hardships they are now enduring. They cannot be permitted to have that."

"Jolly good, our men have beat a brilliant retreat. Those Old Contemptibles of ours are as tough as nails and the best marksmen on earth. They'll be ready. What about your men, General Joffre?"

"They have also had to retreat, but in doing so they have not surrendered. We have not allowed any prisoners nor any of our artillery to be taken. They are ready to fight. Go on. Mr. Holmes."

"The delays have done great damage to the German war plans. They were expecting to be able to take Paris within weeks, and they do not have the capacity to deliver more food, or forage, or reserve troops to the front. We have successfully destroyed the bridges and railway lines they were hoping to use to advance their men and artillery. The advantage is now ours."

"I know and respect your reputation, Mr. Holmes," said Lord Kitchener. "You are known as a brilliant detective and a splendid spy. However, you will have to convince me that your sources of this data are reliable. How do you know what you know?"

"My information has come to me first hand from Mrs. Zelle Macleod," said Holmes, and he nodded to Mata Hari.

"We are acquainted with Mata Hari," said General Gallieni.

"As I am with you, Joseph," she said and gave him a coy smile. He blushed ever so slightly before challenging her.

"Where and how did you obtain this intelligence?"

"Over the dinner table and in the bedrooms of Consul Kroemer, Minister von Jagow, Herr Albert Kiepert of the German intelligence branch, and the Chancellor himself."

"Where did you meet the Chancellor?"

"In the residence of von Jagow on the Potsdamer Platz."

"I have been in his home. Describe it."

"*Eh bien.* Like all German homes, the furniture is ugly. There are paintings or copies of paintings everywhere by Holbien, both the younger and older. And by Albrecht Dürer and one by Rembrandt that he probably stole from the Dutch. There must have been half-a-dozen busts of their musicians—Beethoven, Bach, Brahms, Wagner—do you want me to go on?"

"No. Tell me about this Liepert man. What was he wearing?"

"When?"

"When he told you about the reports from the front."

She did not immediately answer but smiled at General Gallieni. "According to my friend, Elise Vannier, the same as you do when she is pretending to be Red Riding Hood in her scarlet *chaperon* and you are pretending to be the *grand méchant loup.* Does that answer your question or shall I be more explicit?"

"That is more than enough. Your reputation as the most accomplished of our *grandes horizontales* is well-deserved."

"Can we now conclude," asked General Joffre, "that we must resist the onslaught of the enemy with every man available?"

"I still have misgivings," said Field Marshall John French. "I have already lost over a thousand of my men, and we do not yet have reserves on this side of the Channel to help them."

General Joffe stood and walked over to the commander of the BEF. He clutched Sir John's hands, imploring him to support the attack.

"*C'est la France qui vous supplie, mon frère.*"

The two old soldiers looked at each other, their eyes glistening.

"Very well, all that men can do, our fellows will do," said French.

"*Merci, mon ami.* I will give orders for my armies to take their positions along the River Marne. We have several thousand more men camped here in Paris at *Les Invalides* who will be available as reserves to rush into any place in the line if they are needed."

"How are you going to get them there in time," asked Gallieni. "The Marne is thirty miles from Paris. It will take an entire day to march them there."

"Mais oui, that could be a problem."

Holmes looked at the two of them and asked, "Why not use your taxis? You must have over a thousand of them?"

"Monsieur," said Gallieni, "that is a brilliant suggestion. I will send a notice out to have them commandeered for moving our troops."

"That will help," said Kitchener. "But this war is going to come down to our ability to kill more Germans than we let them kill us."

The meeting ended. On the fifth of September, the battle along the Marne River began.

Adieu, Cher Madame

On 5 September, the German army reached the Marne. The BEF and French armies were waiting for them and launched a counter-attack. It was successful.

Every man in the Old Contemptibles of the BEF was required to fire at least fifteen shots in sixty seconds and hit a target three hundred yards away. Many could get off thirty shots. Their record was thirty-eight. They held off wave after wave of German infantry and then began to march forward.

Six hundred Paris taxis appeared at *Les Invalides* and, under cover of darkness, they transported several thousand French troops to the front. None were allowed to turn on their headlights. Their only guide in the long line was the taillights of the taxi in front of them. After bringing fresh troops to the front, they took the wounded back into the hospitals in Paris.

On 9 September, the German generals saw that their lines had been breached, and a dangerous opening in one of their flanks was getting worse. They gave the order to retreat.

On 10 September, General von Moltke ordered all forces to retreat back to the frontier. They were pursued by the Allied forces all the way to the Ainse River. There they stopped on the high ground and dug in. Trench warfare began.

"There is nothing more we can do here," said Holmes, as he, Watson and Mata Hari sat one last time in the bar of the Ritz. "It is time for me to return to my bees and my books."

"And I," said Watson, "shall go back to Barts. So many of our young doctors have been called to the front. Us old boys have been asked to fill in. And what will you do, my dear lady?"

"I shall have to return to Holland until the war is over."

"That is a sensible plan."

"Sensible. I will not be shot, but I might die of boredom."

"Madam," said Holmes, "it would be better to be bored than to continue playing your dangerous game of spying for anyone who will pay you."

"What life is worth living if there is not something to set one's heart racing? What can be more thrilling than knowing one is facing the possibility of death? May God bless the two of you. As for me, if I perish, I perish."

Did you enjoy this story? Are there ways it could be improved? Please help the author and future readers by leaving a constructive review on the site from which you obtained the book. Thank you. Much appreciated,

CSC

Dear Sherlockian Readers:

In writing this story, I have tried to incorporate as much historical fact as possible. When I couldn't do that, I made things up in order to complete the story.

Many of the names, dates, places and battles are accurate as they appeared during the opening days of World War One. The locations and travel distances are more or less as they were in August and September 1914.

The events in the life of Mata Hari have been reorganized to fit the timeline of the story. She did, however, leave Holland and return to Paris partway through the war and continued to be paid as a spy for both France and Germany, and to be a person of suspicion for England.

On February 13, 1917, Mata Hari was arrested in Paris and accused of being a German spy. She declared her innocence but was tried and found guilty. On October 15, 1917, she was executed by a French firing squad. Debates over her guilt or innocence continue to this day.

A personal note on the Angels of Mons: When I was about ten years old, my maternal Scottish grandmother, Mrs. Mary Mitchell, was babysitting my brother and me. As she tucked me into bed, I posed a question to her. "Grandma, how do we know that God really exists?" She responded by telling me the story of the angels at Mons. Many people of her generation had heard the story in their youth and believed it. It was some twenty years later that I came across a reference to it in a book by C.S. Lewis. It turns out that the story was made up and printed as fiction in a British newspaper shortly after the battle and the Great Retreat. It spread around the world as a true story.

The taxicabs of the Marne: Some 600 taxicabs were commandeered to move troops from Paris to the front. That really happened. The legend that the taxis saved Paris and allowed the

Allied forces to enjoy the Miracle on the Marne is highly exaggerated. I first heard about them when the story was recounted by Mr. Vincent Craven ('Cobber'), the long-time director of Pioneer Boys Camp in Muskoka, Canada. In his telling, the legend was true and came alive.

According to Agatha Christie, Hercule Poirot came to England as a refugee from Belgium after its invasion by the Germans.

The cover picture is the real Mata Hari, taken in black and white and colorized. She was really something, and it was fun to link her up with Sherlock Holmes.

About the Author

In May of 2014, the Sherlock Holmes Society of Canada – better known as The Bootmakers – announced a contest for a new Sherlock Holmes story. Although he had no experience writing fiction, the author submitted a short Sherlock Holmes mystery and was blessed to be declared one of the winners. Thus inspired, he has continued to write new Sherlock Holmes mysteries since. He is now on a quest to write a new Sherlock Holmes mystery novella as a tribute to each of the original sixty stories in the Canon. He has been writing these stories while living in Toronto, Tokyo, the Okanagan Valley, Bahrain, Buenos Aires, and Manhattan.

More Historical Mysteries
by Craig Stephen Copland

www.SherlockHolmesMystery.com

Super Collections A and B

49 New Sherlock Holmes Mysteries.

The perfect ebooks for readers who subscribe to Kindle Unlimited.

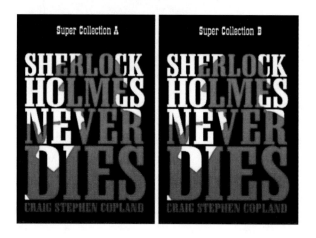

Made in United States
North Haven, CT
22 August 2023

40600266R00115